What they're saying about "Dark Sky, Dark Land"...

When I was first told about an upcoming book on the accomplishments of Hmong children in the United States, I must admit that my eyes teared in response.

Early on in the conflict in Southeast Asia, I was a young Green Beret officer who found himself inserted into Laos... I lived with the Hmongs for nearly a year. They became as my family and I as theirs... On more than one occasion, my life was spared by the bravery of a Hmong warrior.

I feel an immense pride in the accomplishments of the Hmong people in the United States. They have taken the offerings of the United States and made successes of themselves. I feel an immense sorrow for my friends who are no longer able to dream of someday being free.

–D. Allen Mandlebaum, 1st Lieutenant, U.S. Army Special Forces

Once I began to read Dark Sky, Dark Land, I was unable to put it down until I was finished. The life histories of the young Hmong men in Troop 100 were most moving... It is precisely the kind of informed and sensitive cross-cultural and personal approach which has been missing from literature on the Hmong.

–Kristen L. Monzel, Department of Geography, Syracuse University

I am particularly impressed with the degree of intimacy Mr. Moore obviously established with these boys, and the honesty it elicited from them.

–Anne Fadiman, writer

The stories contained in the book are truly awe-inspiring examples of the ability of the human spirit to endure the unthinkable.

–Margaret Robertson, Oral Historian, Minnesota Historical Society

I would rate this book as an excellent work that is required to fill the current vacuum concerning how and why the Hmong arrived in the USA.

–James E. Coughlan, Centre for the Study of Australian-Asian Relations, Griffith University, Nathan, Brisbane, Queensland, Australia

The stories are not only inspiring and compelling, but provide a unique insight into the extreme hardships that some children endure, and their ability to overcome such tremendous odds and become productive citizens in their adopted land. I am extremely proud of the work that Dave Moore has done with these boys and the significant and meaningful part that the Scouting program was able to play in their lives.

–Clarence Hammett, Scout Executive, Viking Council, Boy Scouts of America

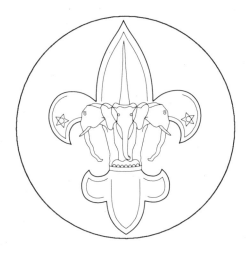

DARK SKY, DARK LAND

STORIES OF THE HMONG BOY SCOUTS OF TROOP 100

by David L. Moore

Tessera Publishing, Inc.
Eden Prairie, Minnesota

On the cover
l-r, back row: Daobay Ly, Xoua Pha
Middle row: Song Ning Lee, Yee Chang, Pao Ly Vu,
Kou Vue, Chue Vue
Front row: Her Lee, Su Thao

Copyright © 1989 by David L. Moore

Cover design by Laurie Montgomery
Illustrations by Tim Montgomery

Cover photo © 1988 Dick Swanson,
6122 Wicasset Road, Bethesda, MD

Published by Tessera Publishing, Inc.

Library of Congress Number 89-51103

International Standard Book Number 0-9623029-0-2

First printing,
0 9 8 7 6 5 4 3 2
Printed in the United States of America

To the Scouts and leaders of Troop 100

Contents

The book you are about to read contains some amazing stories. Back in 1981, David Moore, a teacher at Edison High School in Minneapolis, organized a Hmong Boy Scout Troop (Hmong are originally from Laos and fought alongside Americans during the Vietnam War). Through this association, he learned about the harrowing experiences these young people had gone through to get to the United States. While their stories are ultimately ones of triumph, these boys and their families faced incredible danger and human suffering in their treks out of Laos.

The path to Thailand (the first stop en route to the U.S.) and the relative safety of a refugee camp was strewn with pitfalls. Escape from the Hmongs' own country is extremely dangerous and often results in arrest, prosecution, and even death. And once a refugee camp is reached, there is no assurance that they will be safe or resettled. The camps themselves have serious medical and food problems, and violence within them has become increasingly prevalent.

In this book, David has compiled a set of individual stories more compelling than any fiction. The history of these refugees is, in a very real sense, our own. Although their problems may sound far away, their struggle to find freedom and safety is our struggle as well.

Hon. Rudy Boschwitz
United States Senator
Minnesota

ACKNOWLEDGEMENTS

The young men whose stories appear here were not so much my subjects as my associates in this enterprise. For one reason or another, I did not make use of all of the interviews that I conducted. But all of those interviewed had excellent stories, were very willing subjects, and were very interested and helpful in the project. Here is the complete list of those interviewed:

Yee Chang	Neng Vang
Chue Hang	Tia Vang
Chao Lee	Xe Vang
Vang Pao and Song Ning Lee	Pao Ly Vu
Nou Lor	Chue Vue
Xeng Lor	Kou, Pao Nhia and Toua Vue
Xoua and Xiong Pao Pha	Yeng Vue
Su and Xay Thao	Vang Yang
Tria Thao	

I also took some of the material from interviews my friend Dan Hess had conducted.

Boy Scout Troop 100 is open to all boys, regardless of ethnic background. We have had Cambodian, Lao, Vietnamese, and even an Ethiopian boy as members of our Troop. But its identity is overwhelmingly Hmong, and it is the Hmong heritage that we affirm and celebrate as part of our program. The Troop is sponsored by the Westminster Presbyterian Church of Minneapolis, which also sponsors Boy Scout Troop 33, an old established Troop, founded in 1918, which has become a rainbow Troop for white and black Americans, Native Americans and Asians, inner-city and suburban boys. Some Hmong boys have joined Troop 33 from time to time, but they seem to prefer membership in their own Troop as a base from which they can gain access to the larger American society and culture. The two Troops go camping together, hold joint recognition ceremonies, and an adult staff supports both organizations. But they meet separately and preserve separate identities. Troop 100 would not have been able to come into being, let alone exist, without the encouragement and support of Westminster Presbyterian Church and its senior minister, the Reverend Dr. Donald Meisel.

Camp Ajawah, owned and operated by Westminster Church, has been summer camp for the Scouts of Troop 33 since 1929. Now it is also camp for the Hmong Scouts of Troop 100. It was in the summer of 1982 that they first attended en masse, forming about a third of the population of over eighty campers. Today, Hmong boys hold some of the camp's key leadership positions.

I have been the Director of Camp Ajawah since 1960, the Scoutmaster of Troop 33 since 1965, and the Scoutmaster of Troop 100 since 1981. More than eighty of my Scouts have become Eagles. Thirteen of these are Hmong Scouts of Troop 100.

The adult leaders who, in the past few years, have supported the development of Troop 100 with their time and energy, have given me the utmost encouragement in writing this book. They, too, think that these stories need to be told. They are Bob Fulton, Dan and Tom Hess, Jane and John VanValkenburg, Joe Swift, Gary Haan, McKenzie Brown, and Brent Primus. Most encouraging of all were my two brothers, Stan and Carl Moore, who preceded me as Eagle Scouts and as leaders of Camp Ajawah and Troop 33.

Numerous people besides the boys provided me with valuable information. Most outstanding of these was Dr. Yang Dao, the father of two of my Scouts, a former member of the Royal Lao government and an acknowledged Hmong elder statesman. I spent an evening as the guest of Dr. Yang in his home, and he reviewed for me the last days of free Laos, events in which he played a major role. (See the Chronology for a glimpse of that history.)

The cover photo by Dick Swanson, which appeared in the October, 1989 issue of the National Geographic, shows our first nine Eagle Scouts. They are, front row, left to right: Her Lee and Su Thao; middle row, left to right: Song Ning Lee, Yee Chang,

Pao Ly Vu and Chue Vue; and back row, left to right: Daobay Ly and Xoua Pha. Five of the nine have stories in this book. Dick Swanson also spent a day photographing our Troop during a canoe trip.

Finally, I want to thank my publishers, Tessera Publishing, Inc.: Pat Bell, who in editing my manuscript offered many valuable suggestions, all of which were right on the mark; Donna Montgomery, who saw merit in the first chapter of the book and hunted me down to get the rest of it; Tim Montgomery, who did the illustrations. These three were the first of many new friends that I have made in the course of writing this book.

David L. Moore

A Country of Immigrants

America is a country built by immigrants. People from somewhere else dug our canals, built our railroads, harvested our white pine and mined our iron ore. Years have passed, and now Hmong and other Asians are making their contribution. America needs these people just as it needed its earlier immigrants. Like their predecessors, the Hmong are putting their energy, ambition and intelligence to good use. America wasn't created whole in 1776. It had to be rebuilt by each generation. In attempting to rebuild their own lives and culture, Hmong people are helping to renew and revitalize America.

Dave Moore, teacher and Boy Scout leader, realized that the Hmong boys in his classes at Edison High School and Boy Scout Troop 100 would soon be getting jobs and establishing families, their stories forever untold. Dave felt the boys needed to tell their stories and that Americans needed to hear them.

Senior Patrol leader Pao Ly Vu was urged, as part of his Eagle Scout project, to compile a written collection of some of the boys' experiences. This resulted in a booklet entitled *Dawb Li Txhuv, Ntshiab Li Dej (White As Rice, Clear As Water)*. From that beginning grew this book, *Dark Sky, Dark Land*.

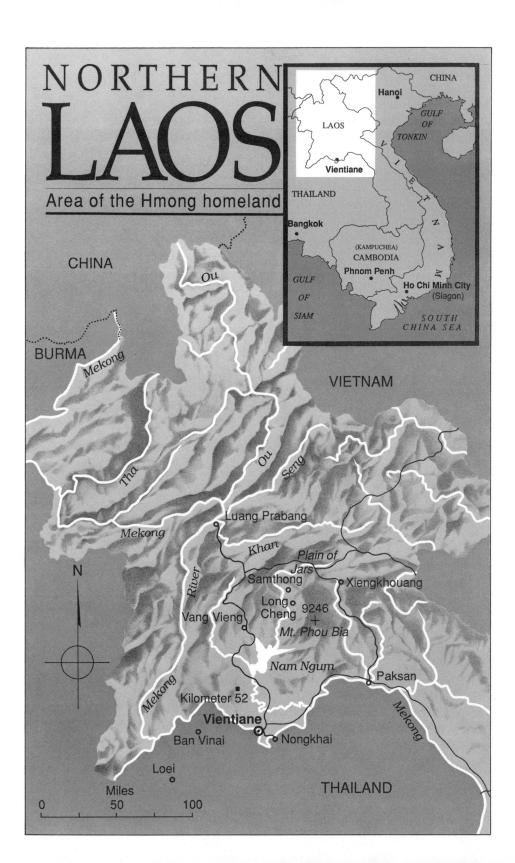

NORTHERN
LAOS
Area of the Hmong homeland

CHINA

Hanoi

GULF OF TONKIN

LAOS

Vientiane

THAILAND

Bangkok

(KAMPUCHEA)
CAMBODIA

Phnom Penh

Ho Chi Minh City
(Siagon)

GULF OF SIAM

SOUTH CHINA SEA

CHINA

Ou

BURMA

Mekong

VIETNAM

Tha

Ou

Seng

Mekong

Luang Prabang

Khan

Plain of Jars

Samthong

Xiengkhouang

N

River

Long
Cheng   9246
         +
      Mt. Phou Bia

Vang Vieng

Nam Ngum

Paksan

Mekong

Kilometer 52

Mekong

Vientiane

Ban Vinai   Nongkhai

Loei

Miles

0   50   100

THAILAND

Atikokan River, Ontario

A Scout is Trustworthy.
A Scout is Loyal.
A Scout is Brave.
—*Official Boy Scout Handbook, 1982.*

Ontario, Canada
August 24, 1987

The canoe was eggshell thin and had a broken rib that caused it to shudder like a wounded creature at the force of each oncoming wave. Chai sat in the middle, tightly bunched in a rubber poncho, holding onto the gunwales. Tou fought to keep his paddling rhythm in the bow. Sometimes he missed a stroke and fanned the air with his paddle when the bow was lifted clear of the water. Then he would be inundated as the canoe dove into a trough. Working the stern paddle, I needed all my strength to keep us pointed into the wind. I knew we could make it as long as we weren't blown sideways. But I was worried about the others. We had to get off these big lakes that were strung like beads along Ontario's Atikokan River.

Ahead of us, four canoes rolled and pitched against the waves. In them were my boys, the Scouts of Troops 33 and 100. They were out of earshot, but I could see they were working hard in the angry waters, bending to the task. No heads were turned. No one looked this way or that. Watching them work, I felt we were going to make it.

Suddenly Chai shouted, and I turned to look. A hundred yards to our right was a capsized canoe. I could see two heads — not three — bobbing along next to it. I swung our canoe toward them, and we rocked sickeningly in the trough of a huge wave. I hollered as loud as I could for the others to hold up and turn around. Tou and Chai were yelling, too.

We headed toward the stricken canoe, rolling and pitching as we took the waves broadside. The boys in the other canoes couldn't have heard our cries against the wind. But someone must have looked back, for I saw them turning about.

Now I could see all three heads: Xoua's at the stern, Yu Pheng's at the bow, and Mariano's in the middle, next to the personal and kettle packs.

"I can't hang onto the kettle pack!," called Xoua.

"Forget it. Let it go," I yelled back.

We picked up the floating paddles and threw them to the survivors. Then we maneuvered our canoe to grab what other flotsam we could, bobbing and pitching in the fitful waters.

"Get into your canoe," I called. "Forget about the personal pack. It'll float." With that, the personal pack went bobbing away on its own erratic journey.

Meanwhile, the three boys had rolled into their canoe and finally righted it. They were riding inside with their heads just barely above water. Pulling the boys and equipment aboard our canoe or trying to right their canoe using ours was unthinkable in the churning waters. Working two paddles against the waves, perhaps they could make it to a nearby point if they didn't first succumb to hypothermia. Though cold and shivering, they refused to panic.

With Alvin's crew now bearing down fast on the stricken canoe, we turned to chase the floating personal pack before it bobbed completely out of sight. Chipper, Yee and Will had already ridden their canoe to shore, and were preparing to receive survivors. Clifton, Chan, and Cam were coming in. We retrieved the water-soaked personal pack, which must have weighed two hundred pounds by then, and towed it in to shore. Somehow, Alvin managed to tow the stricken canoe.

We all crashed simultaneously onto a rocky point. Getting

out, Chan slipped and fell into the water, soaking his only dry clothes. I grabbed three towels and my sleeping bag from our personal pack and ran to meet the survivors. Xoua and Yu Pheng, soaking wet and shivering, said they were all right and refused my towel. Mariano, however, was in shock. He sat on the ground, shivering uncontrollably. His breathing was shallow and rapid, his eyes closed. He didn't seem to know what was going on. Working quickly, we got his shirt off and put him into my sleeping bag. Yee already had a fire going. Alvin found a pot and made hot cocoa in it. As Mariano regained his composure, he accepted some of the cocoa, drank it down, and soon became himself again.

We talked excitedly about our adventure, and were a bit shaken, but glad to have come through it. I gave Chan a friendly punch for getting wet unnecessarily. He grinned and shivered, his teeth chattering.

In taking stock of the situation, we discovered one kettle pack missing along with a new Coleman stove, some pots, all our cups and the shovel. We considered going back up the Atikokan River and searching cross-country for the vans, but this wasn't practical. Darkness would overtake us before we got anywhere near them, resulting in an extra night on the trail. We could push on without much of a problem if the middleman in each canoe sat on the bottom and didn't paddle. Since the personal pack containing Xoua's, Yu Pheng's, and Yee's clothes and sleeping bags was soaked, we would have to build a blazing fire to get them reasonably dry before bedtime. Chipper reported there was enough leftover food, mainly macaroni and cheese, for an adequate meal. Also, quite a few pots, all our silverware, the old Coleman stove and the Hmong knife had all survived in the other kettle pack in my canoe.

When we pushed off again into the wind, Xoua's canoe was behind me, and Alvin's canoe was with it. As we recrossed the bay, I looked back often. Finally, we turned south and lost the wind. We found a portage at the end of the lake. It took us overland to a little pothole. There we spent time looking for the next portage before crossing to Elbow Lake and paddling east down a long arm of water.

By now it was beginning to get dark. We had no choice but to find a campsite. After scouting the shore, we at last found a good one. It was much better than what we'd been accustomed to the past five days. It had level places for tents and lots of fire-wood.

We built a big fire and kept it going as the drenched sleeping bags slowly dried to a slight dampness. At bedtime, Xoua, Yu Pheng and Yee crawled in. The bags still felt wet and cold to me, but the boys insisted they'd be fine. No one complained.

When I crawled into my own tent, Tou and Chai were already asleep. Lying there, listening to their breathing, I thought about the boys in my two Troops.

I'd been the Scoutmaster of Troop 33 for sixteen years and a teacher in the Minneapolis schools for eighteen when a new student from a distant country entered my classroom. I didn't know it at the time, but that was the start of Troop 100.

The new student, whose name was Chao Vang, had been a soldier at the age of twelve and fought in the last battle for his country, Laos. He had faced tanks, seen men blown apart, and been wounded himself. (He rolled up his sleeve and showed me the scar left by a shell that had almost severed his arm at the shoulder). He was carried home and nursed by his grandmother, who gave him medicine she had gotten from a tree. Chao's wound eventually healed, but his country was lost, its king enslaved, and young ex-soldiers' lives were in peril. It was time to leave.

With two young soldier-friends, Chao walked through a densely forested land to the border. The three traveled fourteen days through rugged mountain country, living on handfuls of rice, moving only when they felt safe. At last they reached the border. It was a wide river patrolled by the enemy. On the opposite side was freedom. They'd have to swim for it, but only Chao was able.

He told his friends to hide in the bushes. He would swim across after dark and come back to look for them the following night. If they stayed where they were and didn't panic, he'd find them once again.

At about midnight, Chao waded out into the water and began swimming. The river was very wide at that point, but its waters were warm and shallow. Still, it was difficult to swim the swift current for such a distance. Though he was afraid, he made it across and went looking for a boat.

The next night, Chao returned to his country for the last

time. His friends were waiting, and he brought them away safely. The round trip took about two hours, during which time he was in constant fear for his life and those of his friends.

In the spring of that year, Chao had helped me organize Minnesota Hmong Boy Scout Troop 100. He eventually moved away, and I didn't hear from him again. But in seven years of Scouting, he and his friends had taught me the real meaning of three points of the Scout Law — Trustworthiness, Loyalty, and Bravery.

Yee Chang

CHAPTER ONE

Yee Chang

When the wind blows, it's bound to hit the highest mountains.
–Hmong proverb.

Yee Chang was born in 1971 in the Xiengkhouang Province of Laos near Mount Phu Bia, the country's highest point. His earliest memories are of life in Tong Noy village near the town of Muong Ung. He remembers farming and hunting with his father and brothers. Yee had two older brothers, two younger brothers and a younger sister.

Life in Laos was a round of hard work for the Hmong people. Many trees were cut down to clear the hills. After drying for a few weeks, they were burned off in great fires. Then rice and corn were planted, the rice for people and the corn for animals. If rice ran short at the year's end, people could eat corn. The planting process took most of spring and summer. The Changs often helped neighbors during this time in return for help with the harvest. Last of all, in late August, high on the mountain-tops, opium poppies were planted. To tend them, families moved up to the lonely poppy fields for a month each summer. It was peaceful and quiet up there, and you could see for long distances. Sometimes the fields were in the clouds or fog. At other times they were above the fog.

Yee remembers going to "school" once or twice with his

older brothers, Sia and Pao. It was a strange school. The teachers were young men in their twenties who were determined to revitalize the Hmong culture. They called themselves *Chao Fa* or 'Sky Soldiers'. Unlike other Hmong, they had few strong family ties and usually kept to themselves high up on Mount Bia. They built unusual round houses with "witch-hat" roofs, and if you saw one of these houses in a village, you knew their influence predominated there. They wore their hair uncut to the shoulder. Their leader was Zong Zoua, a name to be reckoned with in the hills. He came to Tong Noy to recruit young men to fight for Hmong freedom. These long-haired Hmongs had invented an alphabet and dreamed of teaching the Hmong to read and write in their own language. So it was that Yee attended his first "school."

The boys and their father, You Mai Chang, went hunting with a cross-bow and a hand-made Hmong shotgun once a week, when there was time. They loved to hunt. It was an overnight adventure, as was fishing.

The family kept five cows and lots of pigs and chickens. They sold opium for silver to the Chinese and Vietnamese traders who came through their village once a year with pack mules and horses. When the rice, corn, and vegetables were harvested, there was a feast. Then there was a long New Year's celebration, the central event of Hmong culture. Yee's father played the *kheng*, a traditional Hmong musical instrument, on this occasion. After the New Year's celebration, another yearly round began. There was no past or future in this life, and no urgency. Although poor, the Changs had what they needed to survive and were content.

Then war came. It was part of Yee's life long before it was close enough to force him and his family to become refugees. In 1975, the Royal Lao Army was defeated, and the Vietnamese communists and their Pathet Lao clients took over the country. As a little boy in a remote mountain village, Yee didn't see, know or understand what was going on. But he could hear the distant explosions. He listened for two years, sitting with men and other boys around campfires in the evening. Yee heard the men talk of what was happening, but he couldn't make sense of the fairy-tale stories of war, battles, and funny-looking, big-nosed Americans.

Then refugees began to appear. They came in family

groups, men and women, old people and children, carrying their meager possessions. They would ask for food, camp for a night in the yard, and continue on. Something terrible was happening far down in the lowlands, but Yee couldn't guess at its meaning.

Then, at last, in about 1977, the Vietnamese came to Tong Noy. They set up camp on a hill overlooking the village, and Yee saw jeeps and observed the activity from below. Now and then a shot or two would be fired toward the village. Life grew tense. People became watchful. They no longer felt safe where they were. And, day after day, refugees kept passing through.

There was no one else in this remote corner of Laos except the Hmong, so it was clear to everyone that the communists were after the Hmong. Should the people of Tong Noy join the refugee stream? There was talk about leaving, but still no one left.

One day the warning shots increased in frequency and volume so that it was no longer possible to stay in the village. People packed what they could and moved out quickly. They joined a refugee camp on a remote hill several miles from Tong Noy. A mixed lot of perhaps a thousand people were living there. They made huts out of boughs and posted an armed guard just outside the camp.

The Changs remained there several days, slipping back into the village now and again to retrieve food or valuables and tend their animals. Yee went back once with his father. He didn't go all the way, but watched from a nearby hill while his father slipped into their house. Communist forces had taken over the village by then, and there were stories of people being shot at while returning. This was the last time Yee was permitted to go back.

One day, as they were eating their noon meal in camp, shooting suddenly began: a few shots at first, followed by answering volleys and then a full-scale firefight. There was a scene of frantic panic as terrified people grabbed whatever was at hand and fled with their loved ones. They ran down toward a creek, stumbling and picking themselves up again. Old people collapsed, and young people turned back to help them. The Changs slid pell-mell down a bank and huddled against the base of a cliff along the creek's muddy banks. The communists were shooting at them from overhead. Pinned down, they watched bazooka shells explode against the opposite cliff. The firing lasted a long time before finally dying down. They waited in relative silence for thirty minutes to an hour as Hmong guards fired a few shots in the direction of the enemy, then they got up and ran, climbing a steep hill. By the time they reached the top, it was already dark, so they lay down, and the children tried to sleep.

Early next morning, before the sun was up, they rose and continued their journey. Their way led downward through fields and out into open country. Ahead lay mountains. As they ran, they were joined by more refugees. Long lines of Hmong, Lao and other hill peoples were fleeing with no direction, just trying to evade communist fire. They passed people who were going in the opposite direction, crossed others' paths and overtook slower-moving groups. People dropped out or turned to go back. For the next twenty days, the Changs ran, jogged, and walked. They tried to stay together and keep ahead of the communists, who seemed to be driving all the hill people out of the highlands.

Days passed with the family alternately running and hiding, snatching a little rest when they could, and surviving on roots and leaves. They ran all night when the country was too open for hiding. They crossed pine-covered mountains, descended into jungle and crossed mountains again. They passed caves where skeletons of Hmong soldiers lay dead at their guns. They ran through deserted Hmong villages, speaking only in silent whispers. Crying babies were given opium to make them sleep, and some died from this. The group tried to keep to the forest and high country, cutting their way through dense growth with knives to form a trail. There were always stories and rumors about those who fell behind to be butchered by the communists.

Slowly the numbers of refugees dwindled as families turned back or became detached from the main group. About half the Changs' relatives from Tong Noy had turned around. There were now about fifty people left when at last the Changs had to make a decision: should they go back or keep running? The options were not good. There was no telling what was happening back home or who was harvesting their rice and tending their animals. The way back was long and difficult. They wondered if they could even make it. Their supply of food was running out, and there wasn't enough for a return journey. Everyone was hungry.

On the other hand, they had only a vague idea of where they were going. Somewhere, they didn't know how far or in which direction, was the peace and refuge of Thailand. They knew little of the perils that lay ahead, but opted against the certainty of what was behind. They decided to keep going and make Thailand their ultimate destination.

One day they heard the distant beating of a funeral drum somewhere in the forest. One of the young men climbed a tall tree at the top of a cliff and looked around. He saw a village in the distance that seemed to be inhabited. Sick, exhausted, and starving, they wondered whether they should surrender and beg for food. They camped for two days, talking and trying to decide on a course of action. Finally, Yee's father, another man, and two women walked down to the village to surrender and ask for food. The women went along so the villagers would know they were refugees and not guerrillas.

The delegation returned with good news. The villagers, they reported, were communists, or at least communist-controlled. There were Hmong Pathet Lao soldiers among them, but they would welcome the refugees and try to help them make a new start there. So the fifty refugees, five families, surrendered and began life in a communist-controlled village. It was half-deserted, with jungle encroaching on all sides. People of the village didn't do much farming, living mostly by hunting — which was why they welcomed the refugee farmers. Later, Yee learned that the area was infested by tigers which had attacked and eaten people. He also saw a huge rhinoceros that had been shot.

Yee's group found their new hosts to be friendly and sympathetic. Simple and primitive, they looked upon their new friends as allies, not against communists, but against the jungle. Even the Pathet Lao soldiers didn't bully them, for they, too, were Hmong. Yee's family worked hard, and in six months they cleared a huge section of forest and planted rice. They raised pigs and chickens. They went hunting. They explored the forest around them and, for the moment, they forgot all about Thailand.

As time passed, however, the isolation of this new home began to break down. Pathet Lao soldiers came and went bringing news of the outer world. Perhaps they passed along word of the Changs' whereabouts to interested ears. The Changs no longer felt safe, and again they thought about Thailand.

One night, two of the five families that had come with Yee left. They were there one day and gone the next morning without a trace. They weren't pursued. Tension increased. The Changs were closely watched; now they felt threatened.

Yee's family remained in their new community until his father chanced to meet some young men he knew in the forest. They had returned from safe refuge in Thailand to look for their parents and show them the way out. Instead, they had stumbled upon the Changs.

A couple of nights later, You Mai Chang woke his son. Yee was told that the whole family was preparing to go hunting. Out at the edge of the fields, they were quietly joined by other families. Dying campfires flickered in the village center. Dogs barked in the distance. No notice was taken as the Changs slipped away secretly into the night, refugees once more. The forest soon closed in around them and they were gone.

Their four young guides, boys about seventeen years old, brought them to the Thai border in four days. It was noon on February 6, 1979, when Yee saw from a distance the river of war, the Mekong. From their perch on a high cliff about two miles away, the river looked small and yellow as it snaked its way through green forest. On the opposite shore, flat fields of Thailand stretched away into the distance. There were one or two small buildings by the river, and two temple towers rising above the tree-tops. Yee had never seen such a flat, peaceful-looking country.

Word passed that they'd cross that night. So, just as it was getting dark, they left the cliff top and began their difficult descent to the river bank. With feet wrapped in cloth for protection, they fought their way downward through darkness and brambles. It took them two hours to descend to the grassy field of an overgrown Lao rice farm. There were water buffalo lying about in the mud, but no people. Between them and the river was a road. Cautiously they crouched in shadow while a communist army truck drove by. Then, in single file, they dashed across to the sandy shoreline.

The Changs had inner tubes brought from Thailand by their guides. They roped themselves together, wished each other good luck, then waded into the river. The water was warm and swift. Soon their feet could no longer touch bottom.

Unable to swim, Yee was terrified. Moonlight sparkled on

the water, and he was sure they'd be spotted. He tried to prepare himself for death by gunfire attack or drowning as they were swept off down the river. Little Doua, Yee's youngest brother, clung tightly to his mother's neck. His sister, Khoua, hung on to her father. His younger brother, Chan, was with Sia, the oldest. You Mai Chang and his two older sons, Sia and Pao, tugged and pulled and fought the current. Slowly, the Laos shore receded. Any minute, Yee expected the shore to erupt in gunfire, but nothing happened. Yee realized he was not going to die.

As soon as they were out of earshot from the shore, Yee's father and mother began calling on their departed grandparents and great-grandparents for help in this extremity. After drifting several miles, they landed on a sandy bank. Thinking it was Thailand, they started to rejoice, but then realized they were on a sandbar in midstream and would have to continue. So they roped up and committed themselves to the water once again. At last they reached the far shore. They crawled up, punctured their inner tubes, and buried them so they wouldn't be forced back into the river. Then the children lay down to sleep. Their parents probably stayed awake thinking of the four other families that had launched themselves. God only knew where the others were, but the Changs were safe – all of them.

Drifting off to sleep, Yee felt an overwhelming sense of relief. But he was also afraid. What would happen when they were discovered? Would they be sent back to Laos? Would they be put in prison? Would they be harmed in some horrible way?

In the morning, a Thai man walking along the river spotted them. He asked for money, and they gave it to him. In exchange, he brought them to some soldiers who took them to a monastery where kindly Thai monks gave them food and a place to sit and rest. Then the soldiers took them to an army post across the river from the Laotian town of Paksan. They registered as refugees and stayed there for two days in a small open shelter, living on army rice. Later, they rode in a truck to the refugee camp at Nongkhai, across the river from Vientiane, capital of Laos. This was Yee's first ride in a motor vehicle, and it made him sick.

Nongkhai was a way-station for forty-five thousand Hmong, Lao, Yao, and other refugees on their way to more permanent camps. Yee's family stayed there about a month. There was sickness and death everywhere in the camp. Young and old, they died like mayflies on a spring evening. Yee became very sick. His skin turned scaly and peeled off, and he couldn't see. He was very weak when they took him to the crowded camp hospital. His mother stayed with him. The family thought they would lose him, but he somehow recovered.

In Nongkhai, Yee caught sight of the big-nosed Americans he'd heard about back in his village. They were public health workers among the refugees, and little boys followed them wherever they went. Yee ran after them, too. They seemed so strange that he wanted to gawk at them like everyone else. He was afraid of a giant black American doctor at the hospital, but the man turned out to be very kind and considerate. Some Americans seemed almost human.

The physical environment of the camp was unendurably hostile. Buildings had concrete floors and tin roofs. The stench of garbage spread from little canals in the middle of the streets where people floated their refuse. All kinds of things were going on. There were rooster fights in some of the buildings. One of the Lao families had a television set, and Yee got a peek at this marvel for the first time. Sometimes a car would slowly pick its way through the traffic. Yee looked at these things but didn't go outside much, for he was afraid of getting lost in the crowds of strangers.

After a time at Nongkhai, Yee's family was moved to Ban Vinai, a camp for Hmongs which numbered about forty-five thousand residents. It was a small city, or, more accurately, a giant village where life was not unpleasant if you could avoid disease and manage to cope with the overcrowding. Some of the Chang relatives from Tong Noy were already there, and more arrived later, so that Yee felt more safe and secure there than at Nongkhai. Yee played games with other Hmong boys to pass the time. Soccer was a favorite game, and the boys played with home-made tops. There was a game something like American baseball, except that it was played with sticks instead of a ball. There were Chinese movies, and trucks would come to set up an outdoor theater on the soccer field. But mostly Yee just ran around the streets with other kids, looking for interesting things to gawk at — a motorbike, an American social worker. They would crowd around an American and shout "hello" at him. As the sun began to set, Yee would run home, grab a few mouthfuls of rice, and lie down to sleep. He turned into a ragamuffin, a street urchin, a scamp. The whole camp was his playground, his school, his world for the day. There was no tomorrow here.

Two or three times a week, Yee's oldest brother Sia taught "school" to Yee, his brothers and some friends. Yee tried to learn a little English. Once, he and his father got a ride in a car to Loei, a market town, to do some shopping. Here they bought black cloth to make into clothes.

Camp residents were issued rice every week or two. They were given cooking utensils and stoves for wood fires. One could even earn a little money in Ban Vinai. Sometimes Yee helped Sia carry water, a job for which he was paid.

For the most part, camp residents spent their time waiting. They waited to be selected for a trip to America, France, or some other country. Periodically, long lines of buses would leave the camp, bound for Bangkok. Some of Yee's relatives and friends would be on those buses. Inside and outside, people would weep and cry, since this was a final parting for many. Those inside would thrust their hands out of the open windows, seeking one last touch. The buses would start up and slowly pull away with people running alongside. When they were gone, the camp would return to its daily routine of waiting.

One day, Yee and his family sat in a bus, reaching out the windows and saying tearful goodbyes. They were bound for Bangkok and America. Some of the Changs and Yangs, Yee's mother's family, were already in America. Yee's uncle in Hawaii was to be their sponsor in the new country. The buses pulled away and began the long journey from the northern border of Thailand to the Gulf of Siam. Yee saw fields, farms, and people as they passed through the countryside. The bus stopped only for gas. After an interminable twelve-hour ride, they reached Bangkok, where they were driven to another crowded camp. It was filled with people of many nationalities who were waiting to leave. For two weeks, Yee, his brothers and sister kept to themselves and waited in a small room.

The Changs were processed at the camp by American medical personnel. Then one night they boarded buses and were driven across Bangkok to the airport, where they were hurried through a big building and into an airplane. Yee couldn't figure out how they'd gotten in. It seemed as if the plane was in the building and they had stepped into it from a hallway. They buckled on seat belts as the plane taxied and took off. Yee was terrified as he watched the lights of Bangkok fade away far below. The Changs were the only Hmong on board, and Yee felt strange and looked at.

The airplane passed high over Laos to Hong Kong, then up into the air again and on to Tokyo, where the airport was a madhouse. No one in the family knew what was going on during these flights. No one who dealt with them spoke any Hmong, but somehow guides always appeared and led them through airport mazes. The family spent one night in a Tokyo hotel, high up at the end of a long elevator ride. Yee was surprised when he looked out the window and saw how high they had risen. They got a good sleep there and some food in the morning. Then they set off once more.

At last, they landed in Honolulu. It was February 1, 1980, when they arrived in America, and a huge number of relatives, perhaps fifty people, were there to meet them. Some had come all the way from Minnesota to welcome the Changs. It was a grand reunion.

They stayed in Honolulu for a year and a half. The family slept on mattresses on the floor until they received beds. For the first two weeks, Yee didn't leave their small, eighth-floor apartment except to go to the store with his parents. He and his brothers just looked out the window and watched. They were afraid if they stepped outside they'd get lost and never find their way back.

Yee remembers his first day in school. His uncle drove him over to register, took him to a classroom, and left him. Suddenly, for the first time in his long journey, Yee was all alone. He didn't understand the language the teacher was using. At recess, he sat on the edge of the playground and watched while his classmates played a game. At lunchtime, the school food was too sweet, but he ate it anyway. Communication was impossible. All day he had to go to the bathroom, but didn't know how to ask where it was. No one came to his rescue. It went on this way for a week or two.

Yee's classmates were mostly Japanese-American, friend-ly but cut off by the insurmountable barrier of language. The schoolboys eventually encouraged him to join their games. After two weeks, Yee was put, part-time, into an English-as-a-Second-Language class. There were Lao students there, but no Hmong. Yee felt more comfortable with the Lao, but still couldn't communicate. Gradually, he began learning English and felt as if he really were a student, learning something formally for the first time in his life. He was in the third grade.

Every day Yee's uncle brought him to school and picked him up afterwards, but one day the uncle showed him the way and told him he must now walk to and from school by himself. Walking home from school for the first time, Yee was again utterly alone and terrified.

Soon Yee and his younger brother Chan began exploring the city. They found parks with pools for swimming. They rode buses. Their uncle took them to Waikiki Beach, and they had a great time swimming and playing.

The Changs joined a few Hmong families at weekly church services. They were not Christian, but the chance to see and talk with their own people was an opportunity not to be missed. Yee met a Hmong boy, Chue Hang, and they became fast friends and went everywhere together.

In the summer of 1981, the Changs moved to Minneapolis to be with relatives. They found a place on Elliott Avenue, one of many tiny apartments in a large building. They eventually moved to an old house on Tenth Avenue and Twenty-fourth Street and, when the rent there became prohibitive, into public housing at the Glendale project, next to Prospect Park.

Yee was enrolled in fifth grade at Holland School where there was a bilingual program for Hmong children. At Holland, he made friends with Hmong boys such as Mingmor Thao and Long Lo. After school, Yee played at Stewart Park, a city playground which the Hmong children had discovered. There were a lot of Hmong boys there in fancy olive drab uniforms with blue and gold neckerchiefs and bright red epaulettes. They were Boy Scouts. Mingmor and Long, who were also Boy Scouts, told Yee that as a scout, he'd get a uniform. So Yee decided to join the Hmong Boy Scouts, and Mingmor and Long brought him to meet their Scoutmaster.

When I first met Yee, he was a small, thin kid. Later, I met his little brother, Chan, and for a long time after that, had trouble telling Yee and Chan apart until suddenly Yee started growing like a beanstalk.

I've gone on many weekend camping trips with Yee and his friends. We've attended long-term summer camp, braved the snows of Minnesota, and taken canoes across the border into

Canada, where we've had to struggle with rain, cold, and muddy portages. Yee doesn't complain on these trips. He enjoys them.

In 1986, Yee became the Senior Patrol Leader, the elected boy leader of our Troop. He's now an Eagle Scout, one of the first Hmong Eagle Scouts in the world. As part of his Eagle project he taught a class in the Hmong language to Americans. While his project was still in the planning stages, Yee had some doubts about his ability to handle it. He thought it would be too complicated, but no one else was more capable of it. He did it, and I took the class. Yee proved himself a natural teacher: friendly, kind and tolerant of those American adults who were so unsure of themselves as they struggled with this difficult language.

In February of 1986, on Scout Sunday, Yee stood before the assembled worshippers at Westminster Church and briefly told his story. He spoke clearly and with confidence. No one would have guessed that five years before, he couldn't understand English.

For the summer of 1987, Yee worked at Camp Ajawah, Westminster Church's summer camp for kids. He was to be Chief of the junior camp, having charge of six counselors, plus thirty-five boys aged eight to ten and their program. It was a job I'd held when I was younger. For my older brother, Stan Moore, it was the decisive job that launched him on a lifetime of service to others. In 1986, Yee's Hmong friend Su Thao had done a magnificent job in that same position.

Now it was Yee's turn. I knew he had enormous personal resources, but I could only hope the job wouldn't overwhelm him. Perhaps it was expecting too much from a boy of sixteen. He would have to deal with homesickness, fighting, name-calling, shyness, hurt feelings, fear of the dark, storms, and deep water — the range of problems confronting young boys who were trying to figure out for the first time in their lives how to get along together away from home. He'd have to show his teen-age counselors, some of them older than he, how to do their jobs. He'd have to learn how to control a group and keep it going. He'd have to make plans and carry them out. Could he do it? Was he capable?

At first Yee seemed daunted by the task, but as the days passed, it was immensely gratifying to watch his confidence grow. American campers admired him, Hmong campers adored him, and his counselors held enormous respect for him as a role model. He vindicated my confidence in him.

At the end of the summer, Yee earned the Camp Director's Award, given to one person each year. It was a picture of a pileated woodpecker; a shy, rare, permanent resident of Minnesota. On the back of it, I wrote, "He has made us all better people for having passed among us." Several of Yee's counselors and campers agreed that there couldn't have been a better choice for the award.

Yee attended South High School in Minneapolis. He played a spunky, funky Benvolio in South High's rendition of *Romeo and Juliet* and was on the school wrestling team.

Unlike so many of his Hmong and American friends, he's always open to new experiences, always willing to try whatever comes along and put everything on the line to see how he measures up. He blazes trails for his more timid Hmong friends. He enjoys competition, the camaraderie of American athletes, the discipline of staying in shape, and the satisfaction of winning. In the Region Five high-school wrestling championships of 1988, he pinned his opponent in less than a minute, but it was enough just to be out there on the mat doing his best and hearing his American teammates and friends cheering him on. For Yee, that, too, is winning.

One day I got a call from my friend Jim Peterson, a Boy Scout executive in Kansas City, Kansas. He was hot on the trail of the Hmong in his town and wanted to see if he could organize any into a Boy Scout Troop. We talked for a while, and he invited me to come down for a weekend to give him some first-hand advice.

"Bring one of your Golden Boys," he said. So Yee and I flew down to Kansas City to organize the Hmong. We rented a van and sought them out. Yee ran a Boy Scout meeting and later fielded questions from a group of interested boys and parents at a Hmong church. His charisma was irresistible in drawing many converts to Scouting.

One night, when the Boy Scouts were camping and everyone had gone off to sleep, Yee and I sat up late at a campfire. He told me his story for the first time. As he talked the fire slowly died until I could no longer see his face. He continued talking for a long time in his intelligent and totally candid way, with me asking a question now and then. When we finally said good night and groped in darkness for our tents, I felt a new respect for Yee, his family and friends.

In the fall of 1987, I traveled to Thailand. I experienced the appalling jumble of Bangkok and the slow, quiet pace of the countryside. In the north, I visited the hill-tribe villages of Karen, Yao, Lahu, Akha, and Hmong. I visited Ban Vinai, the teeming camp where Yee had lived and somehow managed to thrive. One evening, I sat in a little outdoor restaurant at the edge of the Mekong River. Before me was a wide expanse of water and beyond it the dark, brooding hills of Laos. Somewhere among those hills, Yee's remarkable journey had begun.

My thoughts of Yee were interrupted when a barefoot kid brought me a bowl of rice. He was about sixteen years old, bright and polite. Through a Thai friend who was with me, I questioned him. He had recently swum the Mekong to escape from Laos and was now living in illegal limbo in Thailand. He spoke no English and was illiterate. He didn't know what had happened to his family. He seemed to have no future at all. If I put some shoes and a shirt on him, he could be one of my Boy Scouts. He could be Yee.

In front of me, high over Laos, I watched thunder clouds build. Slowly the sky and land below darkened. I kept watching those silent hills until the sun set and I could no longer see them.

Xe Vang

CHAPTER TWO

XE VANG

> The Meo (Hmong) is capable of hiking all day without stop-
> ping, his rifle on his shoulder, descending and climbing the
> steepest mountains with the same springy step; not stopping
> until evening– because the night belongs to Mr. Tiger.
> –Col. Henri Roux of the French special forces, 1945.

Suddenly they were there, hanging around the stairwells
one day after lunch, waiting for the bell, looking lost and frightened. Thrust into the hostile environment of an American high
school, the Hmong were among us.

They nodded politely when I said hello to them in passing.
Sometimes they muttered a soft monosyllabic reply; in what language, I couldn't guess. But mostly they looked down at their
feet, avoiding eye contact. They had their own teachers and their
own programs. They were strangers.

One of these strangers was Xe Vang. It took a while, but
eventually I got to know Xe. One day, he told me his story.

Xe Vang was born about 1963 in Buom Long, a fortified
Hmong town in the mountains on the edge of the strategic Plain
of Jars in the Xiengkhouang Province of Laos. He doesn't
remember a time without war. In the early 1960's, the communist Red Lao, or Pathet Lao, backed by the power of North
Vietnam, were involved in a tremendous, three-cornered struggle for the Plain of Jars with the government and the rebel

Captain Kong Le. Buom Long was caught in the middle. Hmong farmers lived in Buom Long for protection while cultivating fields in nearby villages. Small boys learned how to use guns and became soldiers at an early age. Rice, supplies, and ammunition were dropped from airplanes so people trapped in Buom Long could eat, defend themselves, and survive.

The war for the Plain of Jars constantly shifted the Hmong population of the surrounding mountains. One of Xe's earliest memories is of being evacuated by airplane to Xendith, a Lao town in the lowlands. Unfortunately, it turned out that disease was a serious threat to the Hmong in lowland areas. People became sick, wasted away, and died. Xe's little brother got sick and was sent with his mother by airplane to Samthong, where there were doctors. But the boy died.

The Hmong evacuated Xendith and walked for three days to Samthong. Xe, his two sisters, and an older brother made the journey. His mother was already in Samthong and his father was away fighting the Pathet Lao with General Vang Pao's Hmong army. As refugees, they carried rice, cooking pots, blankets, and sheets of plastic to protect themselves while they slept, since it was the rainy season. Xe, who was about three years old, walked bare-footed, carrying a blanket. It was all he could manage. The trail led up steep mountains and down the other side. It was hard going for a small boy. Xe wanted to rest and drink water, but his family wouldn't let him stop. He cried, but had to keep moving. Many old people who couldn't keep up lay down and died.

At last they reached Samthong, a Hmong stronghold swollen with refugees. Xe's mother was there. They had a funeral for Xe's little brother, wrapping the body in a parachute to make a home for him. Then they buried it in the traditional Hmong manner.

Samthong was overcrowded, with no place to live. So they walked on to Long Cheng, the Hmong military headquarters. This, too, was crowded, and they had to share a small, one-room hut with two other families. But though they were finally out of the rain, there was no wood or charcoal for a fire, so they were unable to cook.

Eventually the Vangs rode an airplane back to Buom Long, which was now on the front line of fighting against the Pathet Lao. The family was together again, and Xe's father and uncle served in the town's defense force.

Boum Long was supplied by air-drops through three or four years of constant bombardment. During that time, Xe learned to carry and use a carbine rifle. Women and children lived in a central collection of huts, with soldiers manning a fortified barricade around them. Their perimeter defense consisted of a six-foot-deep trench with sharpened bamboo stakes at the bottom. Day or night, the town was never safe from enemy shelling. When Xe heard the whine of an approaching shell, he knew he had only a couple seconds to dive into a hole.

Fighting grew so intense, Xe's family moved into a dugout. For one month, Xe left the dugout only to perform bodily functions, cook, and stand guard. Inside, day and night were the same. Light was provided by a single sputtering oil lamp. Shelling was constant, and at night communist forces would storm the town. American planes from Thailand passed overhead, dropping flares as the communists blasted a hole in the trench barricade and came pouring through. Xe could see their hunched-over, running forms by the light of the flares. He fired his carbine at them, never knowing how many he hit. In the mornings, there were dead enemy soldiers everywhere. Since the stench was unbearable, and their water was spoiled, they had to dig wells.

Xe's father and uncle felt they couldn't continue to live under constant attack and threat of death. Therefore, they decided to move out of the Hmong highlands to a place called Kilometer Twenty-five (so-called for its distance from Vientiane). Other Hmong refugees were said to be living there in peace.

Xe lived at Kilometer Twenty-five about three years. In the absence of fighting, he was able to go to school for the first time. He studied math, history, and French and learned to write Lao. The teacher had the only book, so much use was made of the blackboard. Students recited lessons aloud for the most part, but there were occasional written tests.

Early in 1975 the Vangs decided to return to the Hmong highlands in Xiengkhouang Province. They arrived at a place called Phu Lat where they built a house, planted rice, and stayed about five months. The new rice plants were nearly five inches high when, on May 5, 1975, they heard shocking news over the radio. General Vang Pao, the Hmong chief, had fled by airplane. The war was lost, and the country would now be taken over by the communists.

Years ago, before he died, Xe's great-grandfather told his grandsons about the communists. They would come peacefully at first, perhaps, but they wanted your wife, land, animals, everything. Under no circumstances were they to be trusted.

So the Vangs headed south once more. The whole country was being evacuated, and refugees were crowding the trails. Hmong, Lao, Yao, highlanders and lowlanders; all kinds of people were leaving. A few, mostly Lao, stayed behind to take their chances with the new rulers. Also, some of the Hmong men decided to stay in the hills and fight. They called themselves "Sky Soldiers" or *Chao Fa*. At Long Cheng, helicopters were evacuating people to Thailand. It was a panic scene as people fought for space on the craft and families became separated.

The Vangs packed up and left on foot. With young children to look after, they couldn't afford to do otherwise. They passed through empty villages where crops lay untended and animals roamed, crying. They would reach such a village, eat what food there was, feed the abandoned animals, and keep going. In this way, they came to a place called Na Xou.

People were choking the roads. The column slowed and stopped. Up ahead, order had broken down. The communists had helicoptered a respected Hmong chief, Touby Lyfoung, to the head of the column to try to persuade them to turn back. It was the last time Touby was seen alive. Red Lao had taken a bridge and were shooting refugees as they tried to cross. Xe's cousin's wife had been shot in the leg. The Vangs halted to consider what to do. There were stories and rumors everywhere about ways to leave the country. All people needed was money, but they'd have to trust strangers who were not Hmong.

The Vangs camped in Na Xou for three or four days, until Xe's uncle, Cher Pao Vang, told Xe's father he was going to take the boys to Thailand. He didn't want the communists to catch them and turn them into soldiers. If it was possible, they'd meet again; if not, it was goodbye forever.

Xe's father wept, but didn't want his sons to become soldiers for the enemy, so he said to them, "Boys, if we're lucky, we'll get to see each other again and be father and son once more. But now you'll have to listen to your uncle. If I die, he'll be your father. Stay together, help each other, don't forget your father and mother, and always love one another."

Leaving his father to look after the women and girls, Xe, his brother, cousins and uncle set out for Thailand. Their Lao guides brought them to a huge lake, a reservoir called Nam Ngum which was ringed by mountains. They got into a waiting motorboat and crossed the lake under cover of darkness. On the other side was a road. The guide told them to go up to the road and wait for a taxi. But could they trust him? During such unsettled times, even a friend might kill a person, and here they were trusting strangers who weren't even Hmong.

There was nothing to do but go up to the road and wait. They waited for some time until finally a taxi came. Was this the one they were expecting? They hailed it, got in, and drove off, passing by many people who were going in the same direction. The road gradually became overcrowded. Traffic slowed to a stop. Their Lao guides left the taxi to look around and soon disappeared in the crowd. In front of them was a turnpike barrier manned by police. A soldier stuck his head into the car and asked where they were going and if they had papers.

"Going to Thailand, eh?" he smiled. "Well, it's OK if you want to go, it's just fine. You can go. You can see we're not bad guys at all. We're good guys. It's too late for you to drive now, but there's a place right over there where you can stay the night, then tomorrow you can keep going."

The boys and their uncle were led to a one-room hut with no windows. Saying he'd be back in a minute, the policeman locked the door on them. They didn't see him again until morning.

When he returned, the policeman no longer played a good guy. "We're sending you back where you came from," he said. "We've changed our rules. We don't want anyone to go to Thailand, because now everyone has freedom. Even women have freedom like men."

Xe's uncle asked if they could go to Kilometer Fifty-two. There was a large Hmong refugee settlement there, and it wasn't far down the road. They were told they couldn't go to Kilometer Fifty-two, so Xe got to see his father and mother again after all. There was an emotional reunion when the boys and their uncle returned. It was as if they had come back from the dead. Everyone cried and hugged one another.

The family lived for a year at Kilometer Twenty-five and raised rice. They were at peace, but there was always the danger the boys would be taken away and forced to become soldiers. There were stories about the Chao Fa guerrillas and great battles raging around Mount Phu Bia. Should the Vangs join the Chao Fa? Some of Xe's uncles openly questioned whether they should stay there and die or go help in the fight. But Xe's great-grandfather had cautioned them not to join the guerrillas. They would be strong and fight bravely at first. They'd even be immune from bullets. But eventually they'd weaken, and all would die.

In spite of this grim warning, Xe decided to join the Chao Fa. He cut off a lock of his hair and sent it to them to seal his commitment. But it was not to be. A letter arrived from Na Xu. One hundred and fifty families were to be permitted to migrate to the south, where Hmong refugees were farming. The Vangs would be allowed to go. Without delay, they packed up and set out again with all the proper papers, permissions, and internal passports. This time they walked for a month until they reached Phou Nheu, but the people there didn't welcome them. They were checked for weapons and pictures. Anyone who had a picture of himself dressed in uniform was assumed to be a guerrilla and an enemy of the new communist regime. He was executed forthwith. Former soldiers had to lie and claim they were an innocent part of the civilian population.

Although the Vangs had no photos, people of Phou Nheu still didn't want them. They had to keep going until they came to Ban Don. By this time they had nothing to eat and went door to door begging for work. After a month, they were kicked out of Ban Don. Finally, they arrived at Kilometer Fifty-Two, a huge encampment of Hmong refugees from Xiengkhouang Province. They stayed there three years, farming and selling their produce in an open-air market. They sold rice, bananas, vegetables, pigs, and chickens to earn a little money.

In the three years the Vangs were at Kilometer Fifty-two, they forgot about escaping to Thailand. Although not rich, they were surviving peacefully.

Stories of fighting persisted. The Chao Fa held out on Mount Phu Bia. Resourceful and tenacious, they fought on from redoubts accessible only by rope ladder. They rained rocks down on their would-be pursuers and pushed communist soldiers over cliffs to their deaths. Too many government soldiers were dying. The communists decided it would take Hmong soldiers to counter the ferocity and cunning of the Hmong guerrillas. Back at Kilometer Fifty-two, word was passed that the communists needed soldiers. Xe was fourteen years old, but there were many soldiers in Laos younger than he.

Again the Vangs decided to send their sons to Thailand. Xe was sent with two of his friends, Teng Moua and Blia Xiong, to Vientiane, ostensibly to buy salt. They were instructed to be on the lookout for a chance to get across the Mekong River to the safety of Thailand. When Xe and his friends got permission from the village leader for the trip, the Vangs' second crop of rice and cucumbers was just starting to grow. The boys said goodbye to their families, then left by taxi for the capital of Laos.

At Vientiane, they stayed in the abandoned house of a Hmong leader who had fled the country. At night, they went to a movie, where one of them met a Laotian acquaintance. The Laotian whispered that he had a friend who could take them to Thailand.

"I don't have any money," said Xe.

"Don't worry, it's free," said the Laotian. "Just don't tell anyone. We leave the day after tomorrow."

Next evening, when the sun had almost set, one by one, as if walking out in the evening for exercise, the boys left the Hmong house where they were staying. They met the Laotian again, and he instructed them to sleep in his wife's father's house that night. At five o'clock the next morning, they'd be taken to the river.

The boys obediently went to the Laotian's house and lay down on some mats. Exhausted with excitement, Xe soon fell asleep. It was still night when he was awakened by people talking in loud voices. There were communist soldiers all over the room. One soldier asked Xe if he had a letter.

"Yes, of course," Xe replied as he handed over his letter of permission to travel. The soldier looked at it and handed it back.

"This place is not safe," he warned them. "You must spend the night at the town hall and continue your trip in the morning."

"But we don't know where the town hall is," said Teng Moua.

Another soldier said he would take them there, and they set out, the soldier training his gun on them as they walked. Xe didn't know what would happen, but he feared the worst.

It didn't help that Blia Xiong had Thai money in his possession. This was a dead giveaway that they were leaving the country. He had to get rid of it somehow, so he took out a package of cigarettes and lit one up. He was able to slip the money into the empty pack and throw it away without arousing the soldier's suspicion.

Soon the boys and the soldier came to a bridge. Midway across, there were just five of them alone together. The boys outnumbered the soldier four to one, but no one made a move to subdue him. They just kept walking. When they reached the town hall, the soldier took them to a room and motioned for them to enter. After they filed in, the door was slammed and locked. They knew then they were caught and began cursing their stupidity. If only they had jumped the soldier on the bridge, they might have escaped. They had a knife, too.

"You guys are strong," said Xe. "I'm the small one. I was waiting for you to cut his throat."

The boys stayed in the room all night. There was a window, but it was a long jump from there to the ground. Besides, there were communist soldiers outside guarding the building. In the morning they were taken away one by one to be interviewed.

When Xe was interviewed, he was asked, "You guys want to go to Thailand, right? Now tell the truth. It doesn't matter, we're not going to hurt you. Tell the truth."

Xe replied that he had come to buy salt and didn't intend to leave the country. He wouldn't change his story, even when questioned again by another officer.

Finally, the boys were taken to the police station at Vientiane and put in jail. They stayed there for one month with almost thirty people, including the former mayor of Vientiane. They were in a small room with a tiny opening through which they were allowed to crawl once a day, on schedule, to relieve themselves. It was hot inside. There were no windows, and the bare lightbulb which hung from the ceiling burned day and night. Hour after hour, Xe sat fanning himself with his shirt.

The boys had no money for food, but the mayor's family brought some twice each day. The mayor was kind to all and saw to it no one went hungry.

At the end of one month, the boys were told, "Now it's time for you guys to go. But you don't know anything, so we're going to send you to camp to learn." They were sent to a re-education camp for juvenile delinquents. The camp was on an island in the Nam Ngum reservoir which Xe had crossed in his first attempt to escape. He stayed at the camp a year and a half. During that time, he heard nothing from his family, and they heard nothing from him. They feared he was dead.

In the camp, there were five hundred prisoners, organized into small groups. Surrounding the grounds was a bamboo fence with two manned platforms from which armed guards kept watch. Anyone straying within fifteen yards of the fence would be shot. The prisoners were expected to watch each other. Two prisoner-guards were posted at the door to the sleeping quarters. They were not to let anyone out. If someone went to the latrine at night, he had to carry a torch and call out, "I go to pee," or "I go to poop." Conversations between two people were not permitted. When three people talked, they had to shout so that the guards would know what they were saying.

Sometimes, there were escapes made from the camp. If someone got away, prisoners in his group were punished. They were told their sentences had been lengthened. When an escaped prisoner was recaptured, he would be tied to a post in the main area of the camp, where guards would take turns kicking him or pummeling him with rifle butts and sticks. After the guards were through, it was the task of fellow prisoners to finish him off. Many would be angry because he had added a year to everyone's sentence. Some would lace on pointed boots for the occasion and begin kicking him. Those who were reluctant to join in the sport had to do so anyway lest they be accused of being in sympathy with the wretch and be beaten in turn.

After six months in camp, Xe's Lao friend escaped with four others. Two got clean away. Three were caught. One of those caught was the Lao friend. He'd gone home to his family thinking he was safe. In Vientiane, he celebrated his escape with friends, but the Pathet Lao crashed the party. They told his young wife that her husband had not yet completed his studies. They would have to bring him back for a couple more years.

Xe was among the prisoners forced to beat his Lao friend to death, but he hung back at the edge of the crowd, crying. He and an old man couldn't bear to watch. Luckily, no one noticed their lack of participation.

The prisoner knelt before his fellow inmates and implored them to be merciful. "It's too hard to die," he said. "Don't kick me. Just cut my throat." The others began kicking him anyway. It took him two or three hours to die. Xe held his head down so no one could see his tears.

There was a second prison camp on the island for women prisoners. Xe could see it from the men's camp. Boatloads of women would row past, but the men were forbidden to take any notice. They would risk more serious confinement for saying so much as 'hello'. Stealing food was another act punishable by more serious confinement. If a prisoner were sent to pick up the rice for his work detail and a few grains should stick to his hand, he might be accused of stealing and spend time in 'jail'.

Prisoners in jail were chained head, foot, and neck, behind a bamboo stockade. They lay open to the elements in the warm mud. Their backs festered and spawned maggots. During the time Xe was in camp, he knew of only one person who survived a stay in jail. When that prisoner came out, his flesh was white and clammy. Though skinny and unable to walk, he was still required to work, so he sat and cooked rice for the other prisoners.

Xe was always hungry. There were two meals a day consisting of one small handful of rice and a few vegetables from the garden. Salt was always in short supply. Xe couldn't maintain any strength on this fare. His walk became a shuffle, and he shook constantly. Despite this weakness, there was hard work to do. Prisoners went out in boats every day to cut bamboo. They were expected to cut one hundred sticks per day, bundle them together, and roll them back to camp for use in construction.

Some prisoners made baskets that were sold in Vientiane and other towns for cash. With the money, camp administrators purchased rice for the prisoners to eat. Xe was eventually taken off lumberjacking duty and put to work in the vegetable garden, because they said he was too small to cut bamboo. While he was there, the prisoners planted three hills of rice and vegetables.

After Xe had been in the camp for a year and a half, the authorities announced a mass meeting of the prisoners to be held one evening. There were orders from Vientiane for some of the prisoners to be released and sent home. A list of names would be read, and those whose names were on the list would go home. The rest would stay. There was great excitement in the camp.

"Tomorrow night I have one chance," thought Xe hopefully, yet with great fear. "If my name is on the list, I will go home."

That night was a sleepless one. Xe was afraid. He cried quietly to himself, but he was also happy and excited about the possibility of going home. It was all he could think about during work the next day. When evening came, the meeting was convened, and a camp official began reading off the names. Xe's name was read, as were those of his two Hmong friends.

Xe had to be careful not to show his overwhelming feelings of relief and happiness because there were many whose names had not been called. He avoided these people.

Next day, a large motorboat came and picked up the two hundred prisoners who were to be freed. Xe boarded the boat, sat down, and looked back. From out of the women's camp, a girl came down to shore pretending to wash some clothes. As she knelt over the clothes, she watched the prisoners embark. Xe could see she was crying as she worked, and she frequently scooped up water to wash away the tears. The boat slowly crept away, and Xe watched the girl washing clothes until they rounded a point and she was lost to view.

Back home, Xe's family had lived for a year and a half without news of him. All the letters he had written during this time never left camp. They were simply thrown away. His family at first hoped Xe had reached Thailand safely. But when there was no word from Hmong refugee camps on the Thai side of the border, they concluded he was probably killed trying to escape.

Xe's mother couldn't accept her son's death and cried every day. Sometime before Xe set out on that fateful journey to Vientiane, he had planted a banana tree. As the tree grew, his mother refused to let anyone pick its fruit. At last the family decided to give him a funeral so his spirit would be released to join his great-grandfather in heaven.

Before the funeral could be held, Xe returned. He got off the truck that brought him from Nam Ngum to Kilometer Fifty-two, said goodbye to his ex-prisoner friends, and climbed the path to his village. There were strangers living in his father's house, so he went on to his uncle's house. A strange woman sat in the dooryard threshing rice. He asked her where Xiong Cheng Vang's house was, and she directed him to his father's new residence. When Xe stepped into his own home, only his mother was there. She knew him at once, held out her arms and said,

"Come to me."

When Xe's mother recovered her breath, she asked where he had come from, if he'd been to Thailand, and why he was so dark and skinny. It was true Xe was very dark and thin. His hair was cut short, and even his friends didn't recognize him. His family prepared a welcome-home feast, building an altar of banana tree wood which they decorated with flowers and candles. Xe was given gifts of money and silver, threads were tied around his wrists for good luck, and the village elders came to wish him well.

Xe stayed at Kilometer Fifty-two for fourteen days, then left for Thailand. This time he made it, never to see his parents again. It took Xe and his friends two days to get to the Mekong River, the border with Thailand. There were no trails, and thick jungle underbrush made the going very tough. Sometimes they had to crawl to get through. They followed the sun in the direction of Thailand. One night, a scout came running back to where they were camped with news that their lives were in danger, because the communists were all around.

The group split up in darkness to take their chances. A woman holding a crying baby was left behind, since the communists usually didn't kill women. A family carrying too much was never seen again.

Xe and his friends finally reached the Mekong at nightfall. They waded out into the water and began swimming. The trip across took them two hours.

Life wasn't any easier in Thailand. Xe had no relatives at Camp Nongkhai and slept in a cook shack belonging to some Hmongs named Vang. The shack was open to the stars, so when it rained, Xe got wet.

There wasn't enough rice to eat, and they had no salt. To make a little money, Xe would sneak out of camp and look for work. He dug post holes for electric poles, earning three *baht* per day (twenty-five *baht* equal one dollar). He cleaned animal pens, and earned ten *baht* per week cutting trees. But he was always careful to avoid being caught by the police on these expeditions. If he was ever caught outside camp without permission, he'd have to pay as much as three thousand *baht* to stay out of jail. Xe didn't have that kind of money.

At Nongkhai, Xe's family gradually regrouped. His older brother, cousins Kay and Pheng, and uncle Cher Pao Vang all arrived safely. It would only be a matter of time before his parents, two sisters, and tiny brother joined him.

Then one day a young man and woman stumbled into camp, almost incoherent with grief and rage. The man had been guiding a group of refugees which included his wife and their baby son. They built a raft of banana tree wood to cross the river, but it was too heavy and slow for the swift current. By sunup they had still not reached midstream, and a motorboat from the Laos shore strafed them with machine gun fire. The refugees dove into the water and began swimming for their lives. One bullet grazed the woman's head and killed their baby. The guide feared he and his wife were the only survivors.

Xe found out his family had been in this group, and the killings were confirmed the next day by another group that had just arrived. As they crossed the river, they had seen the shattered remains of a banana wood raft drifting in the water.

The Vang group was eventually moved to Ban Vinai, the refugee camp for Hmong people. Everyone there talked about going to America. But to go there, you had to know English. So Xe went to "school" in Ban Vinai to study English. Instruction was free and the teacher was an American, but there were two hundred people in the class and no books. People were very ignorant of American culture. Some didn't know how to use a doorknob or what a bathroom was. Some had never ridden in an airplane. But Xe at least was familiar with this, having flown in airplanes in Laos.

Xe stayed for a year in Ban Vinai. Then, at eight o'clock one morning, the Vangs boarded a bus for Bangkok. They arrived twelve hours later, very tired, homesick, and appalled by the noise, bustle, and crush of the city. Xe thought about the future. He was leaving his country, parents, and friends forever.

The airplane taking Xe to America left Bangkok at night. Xe knew he was flying right over Laos, but he couldn't see anything in the darkness outside his window. It made him very sad to think he was so close, yet so far away. When daylight finally came, Xe was above a carpet of clouds.

In the spring of 1981, Bob Spongberg, a friend who worked at the Boy Scout office in Minneapolis, came to me with a proposal. He wanted me to teach some Scouting lessons to the Hmong boys at Edison High School. It was a wonderful idea, and I reserved a gymnasium for the occasion.

Now, at long last, I met the strangers who'd been hanging around our halls all winter. There must have been a hundred of them at that first meeting, both boys and girls. We had a regular Scout meeting, starting with a flag salute. It made no difference that we murdered the English language trying to say the pledge of allegiance and sing the national anthem. When we finished, we broke into spontaneous applause for our efforts.

We talked about community problems. Many were appalled by the trash around their neighborhoods. One boy raised his hand and said that he had just gotten off a bus when somebody hit him in the face and told him to go back to China. I was appalled at this and tried to explain that America was a very large country with a lot of good people. Some, however, were bitter about the way they had to live and sometimes struck out at others for no reason.

The Hmongs nodded. They understood.

Then we played Prisoner's Base. It was impossible for me to explain the game so they could understand, but we started playing anyway. They didn't get it. We stood there, stymied, until someone suddenly caught on and started explaining it to the others. Soon we were all playing. We relaxed, enjoyed ourselves and had a great time. When the game ended, I asked one of the kids what his name was.

"Xe," he answered. "Xe Vang."

Xe Vang was one of the original members of Boy Scout Troop 100. He attended our first weekend overnight camp in the spring of 1981. Shortly after we set up camp, he asked if he could go fishing. I told him he could try, but wouldn't catch much in the Rum River. With that, he ran off and returned in an hour, grinning as always, with two heavily laden strings of fish. With a reel rigged from a rock and a pop can, he'd caught enough to feed the whole Troop.

Xe came to me another time with a traffic ticket. He was the designated driver of his uncle's new used car, and had been stopped for driving it without a license. The judge told him to get a license in thirty days or face the consequences, but Xe didn't know how to do this. He didn't feel he could drive well enough to pass the test, so we went driving together after school for the next couple of weeks.

One day, as I was about to climb the outside steps of the Vangs' apartment to get Xe for a driving lesson, I encountered some teen-aged American girls. One of them asked if I had come to visit 'Chinks'.

"No," I replied. "I'm visiting friends."

There is an image which comes to mind when I think of Xe. Sitting around a campfire one night, he spoke of how tigers in Laos could sometimes turn into people. This was especially dangerous when they took the form of communist soldiers, and their tails became AK-47 or M-16 rifles. It was possible to escape them, though, by crossing a river, for tigers couldn't swim.

"Xe," my friend Bob Fulton asked at this point, "are *you* a tiger?"

Xe laughed and assured us he wasn't. But I still think he possesses many qualities of the tiger.

Neng Vang

CHAPTER THREE

Neng Vang

A man is not afraid; a man cannot cry.
            –Hmong saying

Neng Vang was born about 1962 in the Hmong village of Phong Tha, near the fortified town of Buom Long. He had three older brothers. His mother was the second wife of his father and died about six months after Neng was born. Since she had been the second wife, in addition to Neng and his brothers there were six half brothers and sisters in the family. That was too many children to look after, so the first wife gave Neng away to relatives who only had one daughter and needed a son.

Neng was raised by these relatives, also named Vang, and they became his family. Meanwhile, his original three brothers all became soldiers in the Hmong war against the Pathet Lao. The oldest brother died in the fierce fighting of 1969. The second brother was killed trying to escape the country in 1976. The third made it to America in 1986 and now lives with Neng in Minneapolis. Neng's foster father was also a soldier. In 1969, he, too, was killed in battle.

In 1971, Neng's widowed foster mother married again. Since she didn't marry a Vang, Neng, being a member of the Vang clan, could no longer live with her. Instead, he went to live with his uncle who was a Vang.

Like almost all Hmong men, Neng's uncle had been a soldier for a time. But he had lost his right arm, a leg, and an eye in a grenade explosion, and his body was covered with the scars of old wounds. He could no longer be a soldier.

Neng witnessed constant fighting at Buom Long, where he lived in 1972 and 1973. For six months out of each year, during the dry season, they were under constant bombardment. American airplanes helped them by dropping supplies and bombing communist positions. Now and then an American pilot would be shot down.

One day, two American pilots appeared in Buom Long. They had been shot down and captured by communists, but a Russian officer helped them escape. The Russian accompanied them into Buom Long. A helicopter was summoned from Long Cheng, and the two Americans and the Russian were flown out.

By 1974, Hmongs in Buom Long knew the war was being lost. Americans had already curtailed their operations in Vietnam and Cambodia. It was time to evacuate old people, women, and children. Only the men stayed on to fight in Buom Long. Neng and his family moved to refugee-crowded Long Cheng, where they stayed for half a year. When the situation seemed to improve, they returned to Buom Long.

One day at Buom Long, Neng went hunting with four other boys. They carried M-16 rifles and went looking for a large flock of birds they'd seen the day before in that area. The five boys split into two parties, and Neng found himself with another boy who was also named Neng. Just as the two of them reached the trees where the birds were eating seeds, there was an explosion.

When Neng woke, he was lying on the ground covered with blood. His friend lay motionless beside him. Neng couldn't sit up or move. He shouted at his friend, but could not wake him. In panic, Neng screamed for help. The three other hunters finally came and carried Neng into town. His friend was dead.

An American helicopter brought Neng and his uncle to Long Cheng. At the hospital there, American doctors opened his stomach and removed about five or six inches of intestine. His uncle sat and cried during the operation, but a doctor assured him Neng would wake up.

Neng awoke to a doctor slapping him in the face, trying to bring him back to consciousness. He looked at the ceiling and then at the people in the room. He couldn't recognize them at first through the veil of yellow haze. Then his eyes cleared a little and he saw his uncle crying quietly.

It was about two months before Neng could walk again. He spent this time at Long Cheng, after his uncle carried him from the hospital.

Everyone in Long Cheng was preparing for the approaching New Year's celebration. But it was not to be. A few days before the New Year, communist forces suddenly attacked Long Cheng. Neng heard their guns at midnight. The attack was beaten off, but about five airplanes were completely destroyed on the ground. There was no New Year's party that year.

Neng's uncle decided he couldn't keep the family where it was. However, their mobility was limited with the uncle crippled and Neng an invalid. They hired a taxi to move to Vientiane, but the readjustment was hard. A month later, they were back in Long Cheng. They heard land was plentiful in border areas where the Pathet Lao and Royal Laotian forces confronted each other and farmers were left alone if they didn't want to fight, so they bought some animals and joined a hundred other families who were moving there. They planted rice and finally began living the life Hmongs everywhere had always longed for. It was 1975, however, and they were living in a fool's paradise.

One morning, when the Vangs turned on their radio, they heard a new voice reading the news. Up until that moment, they had thought the war would go on forever, and that, in this remote border region, they'd be sheltered from it and go about their daily business in peace. Now they heard the war had ended in defeat. General Vang Pao, the Hmong chief, had fled the country, and communist forces were already in Long Cheng.

Vang Pao had told his Hmong followers, "If you know you're in trouble, come with me; if you're not in trouble, stay where you are." But the new radio voice said, "We are the Pathet Lao, and we're in control now. Don't be afraid of us, and don't move away. If you listen to us, you'll have a long life and be able to stay with your families. If you don't listen to us, you won't survive. Your leader has already gone. Vang Pao was the bad guy. He ran away. You have no leader now. We'll be your leader. We have more knowledge. We can support your farming. We're going to have a celebration. If you don't believe us, just look around you. If you have any guns, drop them. If you want to work your farms, go ahead. But don't hide your guns."

The Vangs were stunned as they listened to these pronouncements. Their meaning was clear: the Vangs were trapped and would have to conform.

In a few days, some communists came to the Vangs' village. There were just three of them, young men, unarmed, and friendly. They stayed in a neighbor's house. The Vangs thought they'd better put on a celebration, so they killed some chickens and pigs and feasted for two days.

When the communists left, the Vangs decided to escape. They took what they could carry and fled south with a group of about a hundred people. They traveled on foot for two days, until they passed around Long Cheng. Then they hired taxis.

At Vang Vieng, near Vientiane, the group bribed an official to allow them to continue. Then they turned and headed north toward Luang Prabang. Later, they headed west into a forest. When they neared the Thai border, they needed more food to continue. Two men were sent to see if they could buy rice in a nearby village, but the men were captured by soldiers and forced to return to the group. Now they were all caught. Their flight had ended in failure.

As a consequence, the group was sent to Kilometer Fifty-two, near Vientiane, where the Vangs stayed until 1978. Here they tried to live as farmers, but there was a problem. The young men were being taken away to "study agriculture," ostensibly. In reality, though, they were being enlisted in the fight against their own people, the Hmong guerillas.

The Vangs were aware of a steady drain of people from Kilometer Fifty-two to Thailand. Every now and then, a whole family would disappear, and most of the young men were already gone. Neng's cousin, Xe Vang, had disappeared on a trip to Vientiane and hadn't been heard from since. Was he dead or had he somehow made it to freedom? No one knew. Now Neng realized he himself would have to find a way out.

One night, Neng and about eleven other boys hid in a field outside the village. A group of young Hmongs who returned from Thailand to help them escape told them to stay there until midnight, so Neng and his friends waited. Midnight came and went with no sign of their rescuers. The night hours passed slowly as they waited: one a.m., two a.m., still nothing. At three a.m., they gave up and went home.

Being the last few young men around, they'd been under

close surveillance at Kilometer Fifty-two, and were put in jail upon their return. One of them, who was too young, was sent home, but Neng and the rest were kept under guard in the jail for a month. Their families brought them food, and they passed the time playing soccer in the jail yard. At the end of the month, communist authorities called them to a meeting and told them about their need to study agriculture. Knowing they would be taken and turned into soldiers, the boys had no choice but to keep trying to escape.

Neng slipped out of the village one night with a group of forty people. He carried an old homemade Hmong hunting gun and traveled all night through the forest to reach the Mekong River as the sun was rising. They hid during the day while farmers on the riverbank went about their work. When darkness came, they divided into two groups, one to cross upriver and the other farther down.

Neng was in the group that was to go upriver. With him were his aunt and her two small children. His uncle had left some time before. The group that was to go downstream included the family of Neng's cousin, Xe Vang. Xe had returned from a year and a half in a re-education camp, and had promptly left for Thailand. Now the rest of his family was following him, but they were not to have his luck. They were never seen again.

When Neng and his family reached the water, it was Neng's responsibility to get them across. He wore only shorts and a T-shirt and carried the rest of his belongings in a plastic bag. His aunt and her children clung to an inner tube which he dragged along as he swam. The river current was swift, and it quickly swept the little flotilla away. Floundering in the muddy water, Neng fought the panic rising inside him. Then, in the darkness, he bumped into a tree that was growing on a sunken island, and got stuck.

Neng and his relatives clung to the tree all night until sunrise, then they crawled up onto a dry part of the island where they lay down, exhausted. They spent all day on the island, but when night came, his aunt refused to get into the water. As a result, they spent another night there, though they had no food and were desperately hungry. Again, sunrise found them still on the island, but Neng now had a plan. He swam across alone to get help. Toward evening, friendly Thais sent a boat for Neng's aunt and her children.

As illegal immigrants to Thailand, Neng and his family were sent to the jail at Nongkhai. Neng had no clothes except what he was wearing, for he'd lost his plastic bag in the river. At the jail, there was no water for washing, and only two meals a day, plus a little soup at noon. However, his aunt had some money, and, after a week in jail, Neng was able to buy their way out. From jail they were sent to the Nongkhai refugee camp.

Neng heard from his uncle, who was in the Hmong camp at Ban Vinai. The uncle sent him two hundred Thai *baht*, which Neng used to buy some clothes and shoes. There was water, too, so they could cook. Then they were moved to Ban Vinai, and Neng joined his beloved uncle at last.

Now Neng was happy. There was food, water, and a place to live. Best of all, the family was together again. Neng cut trees to build a house, and his one-armed uncle helped.

Neng took a bath in an artificial lake at the camp. That was a mistake. His skin turned yellow, and the soap he was using got into his eyes and caused severe burns. He tried to clean his eyes, but couldn't help them. He could hardly see to eat. They brought him to the hospital, and an American doctor gave him medicine. It helped a little, but his eyesight was never very good after that.

Neng stayed at Ban Vinai from December, 1978, until February of 1980; then he left for America. His uncle stayed behind, but Neng, his aunt, and her three children made the trip. They came via Bangkok, Hong Kong, Tokyo, and California. When they arrived in Minnesota, it was deep winter. The Hmong relatives awaiting them had brought blankets and jackets. They made Neng and his family put on the jackets, saying, "It's very cold outside. You're going to be surprised."

Outside the air terminal they were met by the full blast of a Minnesota winter. There was white stuff on the ground. Neng looked around in bewilderment until his friends explained that this was snow.

They rode in a private car through the snow-packed streets of St. Paul to their new home. It was a tiny apartment in a small house in one of the city's old neighborhoods. A lot of Hmong people were there waiting for them.

Neng felt lost and confused in this new, cold country. He cried every day for the first week. What was he going to do here? How could he find and keep in touch with his friends? When at last he started school at Highland Park High School, he found lots of Hmong students there, and that made him feel better. But the layout of the school was a mystery to him. Too shy to ask anyone for help, he wandered the halls, totally lost. He often cried when he was alone.

When I met Neng in the spring of 1981, he had moved to Minneapolis and was a student at Edison High School. We'd already had several Scout meetings at the school, and were now organizing our first weekend camping trip. Most of the discussion was in the Hmong language, so I had no idea what they were talking about. Now and then someone would ask me a question, speaking slowly and painfully in English. I told them to make menus for four meals, two breakfasts, a lunch, and a dinner. Their completed list showed the same items for each meal: chicken, rice, and noodles. I started to protest, but Mr. Touxia, the Hmong bilingual teacher, laughed and said, "It's O.K. That's the way we eat." Now there was a lengthy discussion in Hmong: how were they going to get the food? Finally a boy raised his hand. It was Neng.

"We don't know how to buy things in stores," he said.

"Don't worry about that," I said. "I'll go to the store with you."

So it was arranged that I would meet Neng and his cousin Xe at the Red Owl store in their neighborhood. They would bring money and we'd buy food for the weekend.

The next day we met and bought a lot of rice and chicken, a whole case of ramen noodles, and a crate of apples.

Finally, the day of the camping trip came. We arrived at the site and set up camp. It turned out Neng was to be the chief cook. While the others were off fishing and playing around, Neng cooked the rice. I hung around the fire to make sure he did it right, and was given my first lesson in Hmong self-sufficiency. Nobody can or need teach a Hmong how to cook rice. Neng had been doing it since he was five years old.

"Can we cut tree?" Neng asked as the rice bubbled on the fire.

I was about to say, no, you can't cut live trees, but I hesitated. This seemed like a serious question, so I told him to go ahead. I watched as he went into the bushes and came back with a green sumac stick. He slit it at one end and stuffed pieces of chicken into the slit end. He tied it tight with a strip of bark.

Other boys were now coming back and they too proceeded to prepare roasting sticks. Xe showed up with a whole string of fish; an excellent trail meal was in the making.

We all sat down to eat, and I was served first. There was plenty for everyone. The boys talked in Hmong and I listened to the sing-song of it, feeling drowsy and content. They were telling stories about Laos and their experiences there, and I made up my mind I would learn those stories one day.

Vang Yang

Vang Yang

All over the world has heard that Vietnam has come to take over Laos.
—*Wang Lee*, "White as Rice, Clear as Water."

In the summer of 1979, I was looking over the list of campers who had signed up for a session at Camp Ajawah. There was a strange name on the list: Vang Yang. What kind of name was that?

When Vang showed up at camp, he was small, wide-eyed, and very shy. I understood he was a refugee from Laos. Vang was the first Hmong person I ever met, but when I first met him I didn't know he was Hmong.

It was to be more than a year before I heard the word "Hmong" for the first time. In the 1950's, I read about the "Miao people" of China while studying for a college course in Asian history. These mountain people of southern China had mounted a formidable revolt against the Chinese empire during the T'ai P'ing troubles of the mid-nineteenth century. For years they'd held out in their mountain fastnesses, defeating all forces sent against them. Eventually, however, they were crushed. During the latter part of the century, many of these Miao people filtered down across the border into Indo-China. This movement was partly the natural extension of their slash-and-burn life style, and partly the result of their military setback in China. The

Chinese called them "Miao," meaning "barbarians." I later learned they called themselves "Hmong," meaning "free people."

Vang Yang was born in 1966 in a little Laotian village near Mount Phu Bia. In this village, everyone was related. All the forty or fifty families were members of the Yang clan. Vang was the youngest of eight children. He had six older sisters and one older brother. His father had died of some disease and Vang has no memory of him, but he had a mother and a stepfather.

Life in Laos was good for a small boy who was the darling of his older sisters, and Vang had fun. He came and went and did as he pleased. In the nearby town of Muong Ja there were little shops with all kinds of things to see and buy, and Vang spent many happy hours exploring them. But life didn't turn out to be so easy. There was a war, and its backwash grew in volume and intensity until even a small boy became aware of it. The Yangs were finally overwhelmed by it.

There was no radio in their village. News was passed from person to person, and it grew more and more alarming. One day, with war now close upon them, the whole village packed up what belongings they could carry and left. They had no money for transportation, so they walked. They hiked south for three days, taking extra clothes and food to eat on the journey. The villagers walked all day and rested at night in banana-tree huts they made as they went.

The Yangs lived in the forest for a year and a half, during which time they were relatively safe. But the war came steadily closer. Through binoculars, they could see trucks and tanks on roads far below their hideout. Distant planes dropped bombs. One day a missile crashed into a house in their forest village. It was time to move again.

This time, the forty to fifty families headed north through the forest, making a wide semi-circle and eventually turning back south. They stayed away from roads, struggled across small rivers, through thick forest growth and up and down steep slopes. For thirty days they traveled. Vang's brother Youa was the leader. He was young, but he was also vigorous and intelligent, and people trusted him.

It was night when the Yang group came to the Mekong River. Vang was beside himself with excitement. He didn't know how to swim and wished he could just be on the other side. There was only one small canoe for two hundred people, and no one had any experience operating a boat. Nevertheless, the canoe began ferrying people across. It was a maddeningly slow process and the night passed all too quickly. Dawn found part of the group, including Vang, his mother, and three sisters, still huddled on the Laos bank. His stepfather and three other sisters had already made it across. At that point, Vang's brother Youa jumped in and swam across in order to join his wife on the Thai side.

With light coming on fast, Vang, his mother and sisters and the others — about thirty or so people — hid in the bushes away from the river. Vang's sister's little baby was hungry, so Vang's mother gathered some wood and began building a fire to cook rice. Just then, a communist patrol came walking along the path by the river. They saw Vang's mother and began shooting without hesitation. Vang's mother fell over dead, covered with her own blood. Vang and his sisters ran, choking, sobbing, and terrified, trying to get away. They ran deep into the forest. When they finally threw themselves down to catch their breath, one of Vang's sisters was missing. They didn't know what to do. Vang couldn't imagine going on living without his mother. He was just a little boy and needed someone to take care of him. He wouldn't be able to survive alone with his two sisters in the forest, so they turned back and gave themselves up.

Vang got a last look at his mother, lying still in her own blood.

There were about thirty prisoners — men, women, and children. They were made to walk to a town. Vang's missing sister still had not appeared. In town, all were loaded on a truck and taken for a long ride. It lasted a day and a half, until they reached the refugee-choked town of Na Xou. Vang and his sisters stayed at Na Xou for several months, then moved to Phou Nheu. The sister who was missing eventually joined them. Finally, with another group of people, they made their escape. It was even harder this time because there were communists everywhere. It took them a week to get to the Mekong, moving constantly, night and day. They stopped only to drop down from exhaustion.

Nighttime was especially hard for traveling, because the forest was dense. They had to avoid trails, and there was no light. For Vang, the inky black Asian darkness was full of ghosts and other unseen perils. Again and again Vang fell asleep as he walked or rested, only to be shaken awake by a sister and urged to keep moving.

At last they reached the Mekong and made it across without incident. Vang and his family ended up in Ban Vinai camp. His stepfather, brother, sister-in-law, and all his beloved sisters were there with him. In Ban Vinai, Vang went to school and worked at odd jobs. He had fun and was especially happy to be with sisters who loved him so much. But his sisters were soon marrying out of the Yang clan, so Vang couldn't live with them any longer. He had to live with his brother.

When Youa Yang's name was read out on the camp loudspeaker as being accepted for residence in the United States, there was great excitement. Vang, going as his brother's ward, would have a chance at a new life and a future free from terror and flight. The Yangs held a celebration. Friends came to wish them bon voyage. But when the day came to leave, there was great sadness. Buses pulled onto the Ban Vinai soccer field to take them to Bangkok. Vang said a tearful goodbye to his sisters as they crowded around to wish him well.

"If we don't ever see you again, goodbye," they cried out as the buses moved slowly away. "Maybe some day we'll get our country back."

In the summer of 1979, when Vang's American sponsor, Arlene Swanson, left him off at Camp Ajawah, Vang was terrified. He thought this was going to be another "camp" in the same sense as Ban Vinai, and that he would have to live here away from his family. He'd been told that he was going to have fun; that there'd be games, swimming, camping, fishing, new friends, all kinds of things to learn, and new activities to enjoy. But Vang didn't understand any of this. All he knew was that he'd be left alone with strangers. With the instinct of a survivor, he buried his fears deep down and prepared to endure a long siege.

For Vang, the first couple days of camp were unbearably slow. The pace soon began to quicken, however. He discovered he loved to play soccer, and whenever there was a pick-up game, he joined in. Evenings after dinner he liked to fish from the camp dock. He made friends. Vang understood very little English, but other campers and counselors were patient, and the language barrier was no great problem. His sponsor had been right. There was a lot for him to learn here, and he was having fun. But just as he was really starting to enjoy himself, the camp session ended, and he was saying goodbye to his new friends.

In Minneapolis, Vang lived with his brother and sister-in-law. He attended public school with American youngsters and other Hmong children. After school he liked to go to Stewart Park to play soccer with his Hmong friends. He stayed at the park as long as he could and when dusk came, he'd go back to his brother's cramped apartment and try to live in harmony with his sister-in-law.

Vang has a recurring dream. In it, he's back in Laos planting rice in an upland field. His mother is there, poking the ground with a digging stick. She doesn't notice Vang, even when he calls out to her. She just goes on with her digging.

Chao Lee

CHAPTER FIVE

Chao Lee

Old dogs don't keep watch.

–Hmong saying

Chao Lee was born in a small Laotian village. When he was still quite small, his family moved by helicopter to Long Cheng, where Chao was enrolled in the local school. Because he didn't want to go, he cried a lot and skipped class.

As an officer in General Vang Pao's Hmong army, Chao's father traveled extensively by helicopter. One day he and two bodyguards were ambushed and killed as they were bringing the payroll to their soldiers. Chao's father had been promoted over the heads of more senior officers, and there may have been some jealousy among them. An investigation was conducted, and the soldiers who had permitted the incident to happen were put in jail. The killers, however, were never identified. Chao remembers seeing his father's body lying on the ground at the airport.

Chao, his mother and little sister moved to a small village near Long Cheng. When the Vietnamese communist invaders took control of Laos in 1975, most of the extended Lee family left for Thailand. But Chao's grandmother wouldn't go, so Chao, his little sister and mother stayed behind.

When the Pathet Lao came to Chao's village, they asked the village leader to join forces with them. The leader offered his support. Then, when Hmong guerrillas organized to resist the communists, he pledged village loyalty to the other side.

One day, Chao heard shooting at the edge of town. Vietnamese soldiers were soon pouring into the village, killing people and animals and setting fire to houses and stores of rice. The Lees ran away to live in the forest with many other families. They stayed there for several years, building a hidden village. At first they lived on leaves, wild fruit, roots, and the inner bark of trees. Sometimes men went looking for salt in the lowlands. Later they cleared upland fields for farming. When the cut wood had dried, they burned it off and planted rice.

There was much hard work for Chao and his mother. Though he was just a little boy, Chao had to help cut trees, while his mother built the bamboo hut they lived in. Then Chao's little sister got sick. She couldn't recover and eventually died.

Each family had to contribute at least one soldier for the defense of the settlement. Chao was eight years old, but being the only male in the family, he became a soldier. He was sent on regular tours of guard duty with an M-16 rifle and five hand grenades. Sometimes he stood guard in daylight; at other times it was dark. The nights were cold and lonely, and Chao didn't have adequate clothing. He wore only a shirt and short pants, with no shoes. His hair was long, falling below the shoulders. For protection, he wore a crystal amulet on a chain around his neck. He was confident he wouldn't be killed while wearing it. But no woman could touch it. He thought a woman's touch would cause it to shatter and lose its powers.

From his guard post, Chao could look down through camouflaged breastworks to a road far below. His assignment was to observe the movements of Vietnamese forces on the road.

One day, Chao, his uncle's wife, and her two children went looking for food. They slipped back to the burned-out village where they'd lived before the communists came. On the way, they came upon a fence. Chao climbed up and straddled the top. He had just turned to help the others when a burst of gunfire erupted. Chao was hit in the back by a spray of buckshot and fell off the fence. Everyone else scattered into the bushes. Chao crawled into a clump of bamboo and lay still. The communists kept shooting and moving closer, as Chao lay clutching his M-16. Then a big bazooka shell slammed into a tree above and sent a branch crashing down onto Chao's leg. After that there was silence.

Chao lay still for a long time. When he finally tried to move, his leg and back hurt. He couldn't walk, so he crawled down to a stream where he could drink and check his wounds. They didn't appear to be serious, but his leg throbbed and ached. He would have to stay where he was for a while.

Chao lived by the river bank for two weeks, feeling under rocks for crabs and crayfish. When he found one, he'd eat it raw. Later he found a piece of flint. By striking it against his knife blade, he made sparks. Using the flint and the dry outer bark of a cedar tree, he was able to make a fire and cook his food. He was still very hungry, but didn't dare use his gun to hunt for fear the sound would be heard. Slowly, his leg healed until he could walk a little.

Back in the forest village, Chao was missed. His uncle's wife and her children had made it back without him. They thought he must have been killed. Nevertheless, a search party was dispatched to the place where the shooting had occurred. They found no sign of Chao — no gun, no blood, no body. With the hope he might still be alive, they kept on searching.

Meanwhile, Chao moved down the stream to a point where it joined a river. The river grew larger, and Chao looked for a place to cross. He soon encountered a man who had come to get water from the river. Not knowing if he was friend, enemy, Hmong, Pathet Lao or Vietnamese, Chao held his gun pointed at the man.

But when the man spoke, he spoke in Hmong. "Don't shoot me," he said. "Who are you?"

"I'm Hmong, too," said Chao.

Greatly relieved, the man told him there was a search party out looking for a Hmong boy who'd been lost for several days.

"That's me," said Chao. "They're looking for me."

After he was brought back to the village, it took four or five weeks for Chao's leg to heal. Even then it still hurt him. His mother called in a shaman, who killed a chicken and went into a trance to search for Chao's wandering spirit and bring it back to him.

When Chao's mother married again, his new stepfather decided to take the family to Thailand. With a group of refugees, they made the long overland journey to the Mekong River. There they arranged for four Thai boats. Night came and the Lees waited on the riverbank. When the four boats came, they were quickly occupied and launched. Chao's mother, stepfather and uncle got into the second boat and headed out into the current. Then the third boat left. Chao, a family named Thao and his uncle's daughter were the last to depart, but they waited a moment. Suddenly there was shooting. The third boat was hit and blasted apart as it reached midstream. Chao ran into the woods. He ran and ran. When he finally stopped, he crouched down, watching and listening. The night was still. Far below him was the river, but no more boats came.

For almost four weeks, Chao lived in the hills overlooking the Mekong River. He kept moving constantly, trying to avoid capture. He was alone. He had his gun, which he could not use, and wore his crystal amulet. He was lonely and frightened. All night he could hear animals crying. Early in the mornings, the monkeys began chattering from the treetops. Chao watched the river and waited, looking for a good place to cross and waiting for the right moment.

In the forest, Chao used his knife to cut bamboo. He fashioned himself a raft by lashing the sticks together with vine. One dark night, he launched his craft and worked his way out into the current, slowly crossing the river. At last he pulled up on the Thai shore and sat down, waiting for morning.

Shortly after sunrise, a Thai army jeep came driving along the river road. The driver saw Chao and picked him up. Chao couldn't speak Thai, but he was taken to a police station where they took his gun and sent him to Ban Vinai. Chao's family was already there.

In the winter of 1982, I decided it was time to recruit Hmong boys to be on my high school cross-country ski team. I went over to Northeast Junior High School and made my pitch to the E.S.L. (English as a Second Language) class. A group of eager beavers signed up, including Chao Lee, whom I already knew from Boy Scouts. I passed out some old, wooden, unmatched skis, some odd sized ski poles and boots; then we headed up to Columbia Golf Course for our first practice.

The temperature was about zero degrees Fahrenheit, and the snow on the ground was cold and icy. I could see that the boys weren't dressed adequately for winter, but I hoped we could get in a few minutes of work anyway. I planned to have them do a few strides on the flat fairways, learn how to fall down and get up again, and after that, we'd go home.

My Hmong communication skills, however, proved to be woefully inadequate. As soon as the boys hit the snow, they headed for the hills, with Chao in the lead. They spent the afternoon tumbling, falling and taking daredevil risks on the icy slopes. They had a blast, and Chao was clearly a natural athlete, the best skier of the bunch.

Once, when I was driving my van to Westminster Church to pick up Hmong and American Scouts for our annual trip to winter camp, I happened to see Chao on the street. I stopped the van, called him, and he ran over to me.

"Chao," I said, "what are you doing here? Why aren't you going to camp? It'll be five whole days of fun. You shouldn't miss it."

"I can't go, Dave," he said. "I don't have any money."

"None at all?"

"No. No money at all. Sorry." He smiled and shrugged.

"Well, do you have any rice at home?"

"Sure."

"Would you come if all you had to bring was some rice?"

"Can I?" Chao's eyes lit up.

"Of course you can," I said. "Come on! Get in, and I'll take you home to pack."

With that, I drove Chao to his house. The front room was crowded with beds and little kids. There must have been at least three families living there. We went through a curtain and into a side room where there were more beds. Chao pulled open a drawer and started stuffing underwear, socks, a couple of shirts and a pair of pants into a paper grocery bag.

"Do you have an extra sleeping bag, Dave?"

"I think so," I replied. " We'll find something for you."

In five minutes we were packed and on the way.

At camp, Chao's American friends called him "Charlie." One night we threw mattresses on the floor of the lodge where we were staying and had a wrestling tournament. Chao turned out to be a good wrestler and quickly earned the respect of the Americans.

In the summer of 1987, Chao was recruited to play in a soccer match with other Hmong boys in Green Bay, Wisconsin.

He played in the match on Saturday, July 13, and his team won first place. They celebrated their victory and came home to Minneapolis. The next day, Chao was married. It's the Hmong custom to marry at an early age.

Chao doesn't think about the past. If you think about the past, he says, it'll drive you crazy.

Yeng Vue

CHAPTER SIX

Yeng Vue

> So they led the tiger down the middle of the path. When he
> stepped on the small branches and leaves, he crashed through
> and fell into the pit. Then they hacked and chopped and cut
> him with their sabers until he was dead.
>
> *–The Brave Woman and the Tiger*

Yeng Vue was born in Long Cheng in 1968. His earliest
memories are of Phak Khe, where his family lived and farmed
until he was about five or six years old. There were six people in
his family: two brothers, two sisters, and his father. His mother
died before he had any memory of her.

In 1975, the Vues fled Phak Khe ahead of the communists and moved to a small farm. Yeng's father married again
while they were there. After three or four months, they fled once
more, this time into the forest. They lived in a cave for about
three months, until the sound of fighting grew closer. Then they
left one night and walked until they came to a town called Tia
Pang Ze. They rested for half a day, but the communists began
shelling the place, so they moved on.

The Vues walked for two days and two nights to a town
called Lia Kua, where they stayed for two or three months. The
rice they left back in Phak Khe was needed now, so Yeng's oldest
brother and some other young men were sent back for it. When
they found the communists had already taken over, they
returned to Lia Kua empty-handed.

Since the Vues couldn't stay where they were without food, they let Yeng's brother rest for only one day. Then they all set out again. In two days they reached the village of Muong, where they were refugees with nothing to eat. They planted rice, but it wouldn't be ready for a year. They thought they would have to search for food, but it turned out Yeng's stepmother had an uncle living there who helped them.

The Vues lived in Muong about a year and a half. They had just harvested their rice crop when the communists arrived. Again the Vues fled, this time to a mountaintop. There they stayed a month, going down to the town for rice only at night. They had to cook at night, also, to conceal the smoke.

When after a month, the communists noticed them and started bombing their refuge, the Vues moved on to the village of Pha Nong Hua. Within a day of their arrival, however, the communists began bombing Pha Nong Hua. Again the Vues took shelter in a forest. This time they waited for Yeng's brother and uncle to find another place for them. They could only live in the bamboo forest for about two weeks, since there was no food to eat. Finally, they walked two days to a place near Mount Phu Bia, where they lived about a month.

One day the communists began dropping a lot of papers from airplanes. The papers said, "No matter who you are, whoever gets this letter must go to the communist areas. If you don't, all people age one year and older will be killed."

Nearby villages were desolate, and the Vues were beginning to starve. Crops had been burned in the fields, so that they were forced to eat wild plants. There was no salt. Their only hope for survival was in surrendering to the communists. The Vues took their chances and gave themselves up at a nearby communist-occupied town. They lived there six months, harvesting rice planted by others who had fled. Life was hard.

War raged on in the forests around Mount Phu Bia, and Yeng's two brothers joined the Hmong guerrillas there. One day the guerrillas attacked the communist soldiers in the town where Yeng was living, enabling Yeng and his family to escape once more into the forest. After two days, they reached a hut near a field of rice and spend the night there. The next morning, Yeng and his sister were up early. His sister was poking around to see if there were any chickens about, when communist soldiers suddenly appeared everywhere. Yeng cried out in alarm.

His father came out of the hut, and the soldiers began firing. His father fell down. The hut exploded and collapsed. Yeng dove under a fallen log.

In the silence that followed, a soldier called for them to come out or be killed like animals. Yeng's sister was shot as she emerged from hiding, and she ran off into the rice field. Yeng kept perfectly still. One of the soldiers approached Yeng's log and urinated on it. The urine dripped into Yeng's hair, but he didn't move. The soldiers searched the ruined hut for food and money and left, while Yeng remained motionless under the log.

Yeng stayed under the log several hours. When he finally got up and looked around, his father lay dead in the yard with a bloody hole in his stomach. His stepmother lay dead in the hut. Her hair was burned off, and her silver earrings were gone. Then his sister came stumbling out of the rice field, covered with blood.

"They've killed you," Yeng said to his sister. "You can't go anywhere. Do you want to stay with mom and dad, or come with me?"

"I want to go with you," she said.

They left together, his sister stumbling along beside him, growing weaker and weaker. Yeng didn't know where he was going. He just wanted to get away as fast as he could. But his sister slowed them down. The way led downhill through the forest toward a river. Near the river, his sister collapsed and died. Yeng left her there in the path and went on alone. He crossed the river and kept walking. Now the way led steeply upwards. Yeng thought about his older brothers, fighting on Mount Phu Bia. He wished he were with them.

Toward evening, Yeng reached a high place where some Hmong refugees were camped. He stayed with them for two or three months, even though they weren't relatives. Life was hard, and there was little to eat. Now and then some of them went down into the valley to harvest rice after dark. It was at this time that Yeng could sometimes hear the spirits of dead people wailing in the forest. They seemed to be calling, "Where are you, where are you?" Yeng felt his mother was among them.

The place where Yeng and the others were staying was unsafe, so they moved farther into the forest. Finding food now became a terrible problem. Yeng heard his cousins were living under communist rule near Samthong, so he decided to visit them for the New Year's celebration. He lived there a year and a half, but life under the communists was hard. One of Yeng's cousins was a Pathet Lao soldier, and another was in jail. Also, Hmong guerrillas were fighting near Samthong. It was all very confusing. Living in the balance became precarious.

Yeng eventually decided to leave. Since his cousins were staying, he would have to go alone. He joined a group of refugees bound for Thailand. But shortly after they set out, they were surrounded by Pathet Lao soldiers and forced to surrender. Some of the men got away; the rest were separated from the group and tied up. Yeng was only a boy, so the communists put him with the women and children and marched them all away, men first, women and children following.

As the prisoners walked, a gap developed between the two groups. Yeng was in the front of the second group, so he walked gradually faster until he was halfway between the two groups. He looked behind him. No one seemed to notice he was walking alone. Yeng sat down next to some bushes, then moved behind them. He sat very still as the women, children, and Pathet Lao guards walked past. No one saw him. The guards kept moving down the path with their prisoners until they were out of sight. Yeng was free.

After that, Yeng went back to live with his cousins near Samthong. Life continued to be hard, but encouraging reports were filtering back from Thailand. Yeng heard that one of his brothers had safely escaped, and there were people around who would take you to Thailand for money. Finally, Yeng and the other Vue family members decided to attempt a getaway. One night they left with a group of about a hundred people. They walked for two days and nights, then began resting during the nights.

There were four guides: three Hmongs and one Lao. Yeng carried rice on his back and had no shoes or extra clothes. They stayed off the trails for fear of traps, mines, or capture. Even so, people were hurt. Yeng cut his foot badly on a pointed bamboo stick, but he kept going.

The way led up and down, over several mountains. At one point, the group had to leave an old man behind because he could no longer walk. They gave him opium and left him to die. After four or five weeks of walking, they descended to the Mekong River one night. There were too many of them, so they divided into three groups for their final dash. The first group disappeared quietly into the night, single file. Then the second group followed. All was quiet.

Suddenly, near the river ahead, lights came on and shooting began. Yeng could hear people screaming. The shooting lasted a long time before dying away. Yeng waited. His group slowly began to move, cautiously at first, but then they began running in a panic. There was no order. People stumbled, fell, got up, and fell again.

Yeng didn't know how to swim, but he carried a bamboo life jacket he had made with his knife a few days earlier. When he reached the river, he plunged in, but his life jacket didn't work. Yeng was too heavy, and the bamboo sank under his weight. Just then, someone spotted some boats on the river. Yeng squinted into the darkness. He could see several small canoes, each manned by two Thai boatmen.

When the canoes got close enough, Yeng leapt into one of them. The boatmen turned it around immediately and headed for the Thai shore. When they got to the middle of the river, the boatmen put down their paddles and questioned him: did he have any money or valuables? He had a knife hidden under his shirt, but that was all. They searched him and took it.

The boatmen brought Yeng to the Thai shore, turned around and went back for more people. He knew he was in Thailand, because if he faced upstream, the river was flowing past his right side. But it was dark, and he was alone. Soon he met a friendly Thai man who showed him a place where he could spend the night under a house-on-stilts. Yeng sat there and tried to sleep as the shooting continued all night across the river in Laos.

In the morning, Yeng walked along the river bank looking for people he knew among the refugees who had arrived the night before. He found his cousin Kou and Kou's whole family. Kou had spent the night separated from them, but now they were together again. Yeng joined this family.

Yeng stayed for a year at Ban Vinai, the Hmong refugee camp in Thailand. His brother had arrived there ahead of him, and together, they waited for their turn to emigrate to the U.S.

In June of 1985, Yeng Vue graduated from Edison High School in Minneapolis. I attended the graduation ceremony, which was held outdoors on the football field. I sat in the bleachers as the students' names were read and they filed up to receive their diplomas. Each time a name was read, that student's friends and family cheered. Sometimes their cheering was loud and prolonged. When Yeng's name was read, there were no cheers. No one seemed to notice him as he walked up in silence and took his diploma.

When the ceremony came to an end, the students gave a final cheer, threw their caps into the air, and began dispersing to find their families. I rose from my place, ran down the steps, vaulted the wire fence that separated the bleachers from the field, and went looking for Yeng. I found him standing in his cap and gown, holding his diploma. He looked glassy-eyed and lost in the crowd of American high school students and their well-wishers. I went up to him and shook his hand.

"I've made a lot of money working in America," Yeng once told me. "When I die, I hope my brother burns some of it for me."

Yeng would like to go back to Laos some day. Not to farm again, or to help rebuild or bring knowledge from the Western world. He thinks he can identify the men who killed his family. He would hunt them down and kill them one by one, like animals.

Xeng Lor

CHAPTER SEVEN

Xeng Lor

> We felt terribly lonely because our family had never split up
> and separated like this before. Life was very different when we
> came to the United States. We didn't know what this country
> would look like. We felt very frightened and worried about
> what would happen to us. We worried about the language and
> where we could stay or live.
>
> –*Nou Lor,* Edison Record

Xeng Lor was born around 1961 in the Hmong village of
Muong Ngat. From as far back as his memory can reach, there
were airplanes overhead and the echoes of distant bombing. The
Vietnamese came too close in 1965, so Xeng's family left one
night with a hundred other villagers. They slept in a cave, then
walked to a place called Xa Nya in the morning. There Xeng's
mother tended crops of rice, corn, peppers and ginger while his
father served as a soldier. Before the year was out and the harvest completed, the Lors moved to the top of a large, burned-
over mountain, with few trees and no food. To survive, the Lor
family had to eat the leaves and roots of wild plants.

One of the men had a two-way radio which he used to
contact airplanes. Soon they were flying overhead and dropping
hundred-pound bags of rice. It was a dangerous business. Xeng
hid under a tree after he was almost hit by a bag.

After two days, six helicopters came to pick people up.
The men, including Xeng's father, stayed on to continue fighting,

but women and children were evacuated. They were brought to a place called Ta Pa, where Xeng lived for two or three years. In this village, Xeng's brother and sister died. They both died on the same day, his sister in the morning, his brother in the afternoon.

When the war came closer, Xeng's father moved his family to Long Cheng. There the Vietnamese attacked the airport one night, so the Lor family set out on foot once more as part of a large group. From Long Cheng, they followed a long, rugged trail to a place called Na Yang, near the relative safety of Phak Khe. Though it was already two months into the growing season, Xeng's father planted rice and corn before going away to fight. It was very hard for Xeng's mother to tend the farm, build necessary housing, and care for the children. His father made periodic visits and did what he could, but it was not enough.

In 1974, Xeng's father moved the family to unfarmed land around the village of Muong Ah. The forest was thick there, and, for a couple years, crops of rice and corn grew abundantly. People helped each other build temporary bamboo houses. Xeng's father helped, then went looking for a good place to plant rice. Forest land was cleared, and the brush burned off. The sky was darkened by smoke for days.

About this time, news came that General Vang Pao had left the country. In the confusion that followed, no one knew what was going to happen. Then Xeng's mother became sick. She grew rapidly worse and died, leaving Xeng to raise his four-month-old brother. There was no milk for the baby, so Xeng fed him rice-water soup. Moreover, there were chickens, ducks, pigs, and three water buffaloes to care for. Xeng worked each day in the fields and cut wood for the kitchen fire. Before going to bed each night, he readied food for the morning. He cried often for his mother. Whenever he saw a banana tree she had planted, he thought about her, missed her and cried.

Xeng's father remarried a year later. The new stepmother was always angry and had little time for her stepchildren. Xeng continued to raise his brother. They slept together, and Xeng made rice soup for the little boy.

In 1977, the Lors left Muong Ah to hide in the forest. Xeng was given a gun and scheduled for regular guard duty. He and six other soldiers spent every other week on a mountaintop, three hours away from where their families were hiding. From this vantage-point, they could see far down into the valley. They watched the roads below and reported the movement of traffic. Sometimes they went down to the roads and examined the tracks carrying enemy soldiers. There were indications that the Vietnamese were strengthening their forces in the mountains, but the Hmongs remained out of sight and refrained from using their weapons.

Meanwhile, the villagers stayed in the forest and kept moving to avoid being discovered. They sometimes stole back to work the fields around Muong Ah, but this was extremely dangerous. There wasn't enough food, so they ate leaves and roots and hunted with traps. They cooked only at night. Salt was unobtainable. Without it, they felt weak and tired.

Whenever they went anywhere, they were careful to obliterate their tracks as they returned. Xeng had no shoes, but his feet were hard and tough. Aside from the weakness caused by a poor diet, life in the forest kept him healthy.

In February of 1979, the Lors were visited by some young men who had returned from a refuge in Thailand. They offered to show Xeng's family the way there, and the Lors decided to escape. They packed their necessities and set out on the long walk that would take them to Thailand.

Xeng was now about seventeen or eighteen years old. He carried a gun, a blanket, and fifty pounds of rice on his back. He had to be very careful where he stepped because the trails had been mined. He dared to step only in the footprint of the person ahead of him.

The way led up and down mountains. Sometimes they had to pull themselves up with ropes. But the danger was greatest in valleys, where there might be roads to cross. Roads were patrolled, and pathways approaching them were sometimes mined. They crossed roads only at night and avoided all human habitations.

One day they looked down from a mountain height on the Mekong River. When darkness came, they descended to the river bank, crossing fields and a road, and waded into the water. Some of the group had small rafts made of banana wood or bamboo. The Lors had four inflated ring buoys which their guides had brought from Thailand. These flotation devices cost the Lors two silver bars, surely a king's ransom.

The river was wide and black. They hadn't been in it long

when the moon began to rise. Then Xeng noticed people moving about on the Lao side he had just left. There was a burst of gunfire that lasted for a few seconds. Then there was silence. No one seemed to have been hit.

Xeng's youngest brother started to slip. Since the boy couldn't swim, he had been tied onto Xeng's back. But Xeng could feel him sliding slowly into the water. Then he started choking.

Xeng stopped swimming and tried to hold his brother up. Soon he heard the sound of splashing in the water nearby. Not knowing what it was, he broke the silence and called out.

Xeng's father's voice answered, "It's me."

"Get over here quickly," Xeng replied.

Suddenly there was a desperate thrashing in the water. Another of Xeng's brothers was in trouble. A plastic bag tied with a rubber band which he'd been using for flotation had suddenly burst, and the boy was drowning. Xeng and his father got to him and held him up, too.

Somehow, they managed to tie Xeng's little brother more securely to his back. With his left arm around the other brother, Xeng still had his right arm free for swimming. After a long time in the water, Xeng's bare feet touched something.

"Put your feet down," he called to his father. "Can you feel something?"

"It's sand!" his father called back. "I think we've made it."

In the darkness several yards in front of him, Xeng could vaguely see the forms of standing people. "Vietnamese or Thai?" he shouted.

A voice replied in Thai, "It's Thailand, come on!"

Xeng walked up out of the river, his youngest brother bound to his back. The little boy was shivering uncontrollably and breathing in shallow gasps. A Thai man cut the rope with a knife and took him away. Xeng was afraid for his brother, but he was too weak to do anything. He collapsed in front of a fire that had apparently been built for them. When the little brother was brought back, he was breathing normally.

"Are you hungry?" someone asked.

They were given food to eat and slept in a big house that night. The next morning the headman of the town came to see them. They were given clothes. No one tried to take their silver. Police came to check them and took their knives and some opium.

About a hundred and fifty people had crossed that night. All but one woman had made it. No one knew what happened to her. She must have drowned or been shot in the water.

A truck picked them up and brought them to the temporary camp at Nongkhai. There were about a thousand people there, crowded into a small space with nothing to do. People just sat around or slept. It was very hot, and at night there were swarms of mosquitoes. The shelters had roofs, but no walls.

Eventually the Lors were able to move to the permanent camp at Nongkhai, then on to Ban Vinai. Xeng's youngest brother was weak from malnutrition and couldn't walk. At Ban Vinai, Xeng got him into a program where he received milk three times a day. After three months, he started walking again.

People in the camp were signing up to go to America. Xeng thought they should go too, but his father was afraid. He was too old, he said, and it would be too hard for him to learn English and adjust to strange ways. He told Xeng to forget about going to America. But Xeng still wanted to go. When he thought about his future he thought about America. He wanted more than anything to go there.

Xeng went to the central office at Ban Vinai and asked to be put on the list of those requesting admission to America. He signed his name, but didn't tell his father what he had done.

Six months passed and Xeng heard nothing more about his request. All this time, he kept to himself the knowledge that his name was on a list somewhere, moving slowly from desk to desk and office to office, toward the top of the column for release and a new future in a new land.

Then, on June 23, 1980, Xeng got word that he was accepted. An American in Omaha, Nebraska, had agreed to be his sponsor. Xeng would leave in three days. He walked home from the camp Post Office, where he'd seen his name posted. When he reached home, he sat down next to his father and told him the news.

Xeng's father just sat there, not knowing what to say. He needed his son's help. His son's heart, however, was set on getting out of the refugee camp, getting an education, and starting a real life of hope and promise. How could a father oppose that? He said nothing; there was nothing he could say.

The next day, by way of reply to his son, the father

bought a pig and held a party to celebrate Xeng's future and say good-bye. All of Xeng's friends came. Xeng was excited, though he knew he was seeing his family and friends for perhaps the last time. He was leaving his country for the other side of the world. This made him very sad.

Xeng and his nephew Nou Lor took the long, twelve-hour bus ride to Bangkok. Xeng might have been seventeen, but said he was eighteen so he could travel without a guardian and pose as the guardian for Nou, who was fourteen or fifteen.

When Nou Lor was about five years old, his father got sick and died, his mother remarried and moved away to another clan, and his brothers and sisters were split up among Lor relatives. When he got to Ban Vinai, Nou learned that his mother had already left the country and was in America with her new family. Nou wanted to join his mother in America, but his adopted family had applied to go to France. After a long discussion, Nou was allowed to apply for admission to America.

Now the two boys, Xeng and Nou, were traveling together on their own, their families fragmented and scattered to the wind. When Xeng and Nou landed at the airport in Omaha, Nebraska, there was no one there to meet them. They walked around the airport until they noticed an American man watching them. Xeng wondered if this man could be their sponsor. Then the man spoke.

"Are you Xeng?" the man asked.

"Yes!"

"Nou?"

"Yes!"

After welcoming the boys to America, the man took them to a large, furnished house and showed them around. He showed them how to turn on the heat, how the stove worked, and where to take a shower. There was chicken and other food in the refrigerator, and a bunch of bananas in the cupboard. The man gave each of the boys a key. He told them to lock the door when they left and keep the keys with them. Twenty minutes later, he left.

After cooking a meal of chicken, Xeng and Nou looked around for a place to sleep. The big empty house was frightening, and Nou felt more secure in the basement, so they carried mattresses down there and slept.

Next day the boys walked around outside, exploring the

neighborhood. In the afternoon, their sponsor came to take them shopping. He bought them a soccer ball to play with.

There were other Hmongs living in Omaha, but they were busy working and doing things with their families. Xeng and Nou didn't see much of them.

Xeng had a hard time communicating with his sponsor, so they found that it helped to write things down. Then they could read each other's writing.

After a few days in Omaha, Xeng told his sponsor they wanted to live with their relatives in Minneapolis. The sponsor arranged for their transportation. When it came time to leave, he took them to the bus station. At the station, he asked them, "What about your TV set and the other furniture at your house? It's yours, you know. Everything in the house is yours. My church gave it to you."

Xeng hadn't realized this, but the sponsor said he'd arrange to have it all shipped to Minneapolis. He got on the bus with them and said something to a woman passenger, who nodded and smiled at them. Then he shook their hands and left. Finally, the bus pulled out of the station.

It was an eight-hour ride from Omaha to Minneapolis. Around noon, the bus stopped and all the people got out. At first, Xeng didn't know why they were getting out. Then the driver asked them if they wanted some lunch.

"It's OK. We can stay here," Xeng replied, and they sat and waited.

After about half an hour, people started returning. Four hours later, they were in Minneapolis.

I met Xeng at Edison High School in the spring of 1981. He was officially eighteen years old, but his Hmong friends told him he'd better go to high school, so he came to Edison and joined our Hmong Boy Scout Troop there. We held a Troop election that summer, and Xeng won. He became our first Senior Patrol Leader, the boy leader of the Troop.

That summer, as usual, I was working as director of Camp Ajawah. Every Friday, I would commute to Minneapolis to be part of the Hmong Scout meeting at Stewart Park. I got the idea it would be nice to invite the Hmongs for a day of camping, swimming, and boating at Ajawah. The camp cook, Mike O'Neal, was receptive, but skeptical. How could we possibly fit thirty more people into the Mess Hall for a meal? He thought about it, decided it was worth a try, and we arranged for the Hmong boys to pay us a visit.

When the day came, I drove the thirty-passenger camp bus to Minneapolis to pick them up. Right away there was a problem. There were fifty-six Hmongs waiting for me. They counted themselves off in the sing-song cadence of their language. I caught Xe Vang's eye as he said, "*Plau-chow chee,* [forty-five]" and grinned at me. Then they squeezed onto the bus, three to a seat. Somehow, everyone found a place. Xeng sat next to me on an overturned waste basket. It was a long, uncomfortable ride, but no one complained.

That afternoon, Camp Ajawah was attacked by an army of energetic Hmongs. The rope swings, volley-ball court, foosball and ping-pong tables, and badminton equipment were all in full use. The babble of a new tongue was everywhere. We had to be very careful to explain our eight-defense swimming program, but soon Hmong kids were doing back flips into the water. Each canoe or boat that went out had a qualified counselor in it, and all of them went out. At dinner-time, we crowded into the Mess Hall, twelve to each eight-person table. When Assistant Camp Director Bob Fulton walked into the Headquarters Cabin that evening, the cries of active Hmongs were ringing in the air. Bob had an ear-to-ear grin on his face. I knew then that the Hmongs were with us to stay, and that Camp Ajawah would never again be the same. Later, Mike O'Neal, the cook, commented that it had been a well-conceived and well-executed idea to invite the Hmongs to camp.

Toward the end of that year, after we had been organized and operating for some time, I decided it would be a good idea to present a "Good Scout Cup" to a Troop 100 Scout to be chosen annually by his fellows. I bought a silver cup for the occasion, but what should I have engraved on it?

I looked through a Hmong-English dictionary for some appropriate proverb or saying. Hmong isn't really a written language, but about a generation ago, French missionary priests developed one based on Roman letters. Looking through the dictionary, I finally found a saying I liked: "In good times and in bad times, we are always Hmong." I thought I could modify it to read: "In good times and in bad times — Trustworthy, Loyal, Brave." I thought that described the Hmong Scouts pretty well.

I looked through the dictionary to find Hmong translations for "trustworthy," "loyal" and "brave," but there was nothing. I stopped Xeng in the hall at Edison the next day as he was hurrying to a class. When I told him what I was looking for, he was baffled. He'd never heard those words in English or in Hmong. Could I please explain them?

"If you promise you'll do something and you keep your word no matter what, you are trustworthy," I explained. "If you stick by your friends no matter what, you are loyal. And if you're afraid to do something, but you do it anyway, you are brave."

Now he understood, but he still couldn't think of any Hmong words to fit these strange concepts. Suddenly the school bell rang. Now Xeng was late for class. I walked with him to his classroom and told the teacher Xeng had been talking with me, and I wasn't paying attention to the time.

"Oh, that's all right. I trust Xeng," the teacher said.

I turned to Xeng and held up a forefinger. "Example number one, you're trustworthy."

I went to the Hmong bilingual teacher and to the bilingual aide at Edison, but they couldn't help. It seemed the words did not exist in Hmong, not even the concepts. So I gave up, partly. The engraving on the Good Scout Cup reads: "*Sib hawv zoo, sib hawv pem - Trustworthy, Loyal, Brave.*"

By vote of his fellow Scouts, Xeng Lor won the Good Scout Cup for 1982.

Blong Xiong

CHAPTER EIGHT

Blong Xiong

What makes up a family is not the number of people or whether they are related by blood. It is the way they care for each other, share with each other.
     –Official Boy Scout Handbook, 1979

Swimming and boating were over for the day, and campers were picking up their towels, stepping into their sandals, and heading up the path toward the tent lines. I was going around picking up lost stuff when I realized a small boy was standing by the canoe racks watching me and waiting to get my attention. It was little Blong. What could possibly be on his mind? I feared the worst. For the time being I kept walking around, going over in my head just what I would say to him when he spoke to me.

Blong Xiong was the newest, tiniest Scout in the Hmong Troop. Just how much English he understood, I didn't know, because he spoke so seldom. He never smiled and was extremely shy.

A few weeks earlier, I had gone over to his apartment in Minneapolis and signed him up for camp. He lived there with his mother, father, and younger brothers and sisters. There wasn't a stick of furniture in the front room, so we sat on the bare floor to fill out papers. When I asked him what he was going to do for the rest of the summer, he answered, "Just stay home."

Now we'd been in camp for three days, and it was "dry-creek" time, that moment when the elation of the first couple of days has worn off and life settles into its routine. For old-timers, this can be a relaxing moment; when you take a long sigh, your mind clears, and you slip into summer as if putting on an old pair of shoes. But for newcomers, it can be tough. The days stretch ahead, dull and tedious, and the camp seems to be doing nothing, going nowhere, running like a dry creek. Now here was little Blong, waiting to talk to me. I could guess what he might say.

This was the first summer we had Hmongs in camp, except for Vang Yang a couple of years before. There were about thirty of them, a large percentage of the camp population, and there was every indication that they were going to be excellent campers. They seemed to take to camp activities like fish to water. They were good-natured and friendly, and endured hardship without complaining. Yet, some of them had started asking innocuous little questions like, "When is camp going to be over?" and, "How much longer are we going to be here?" Straws were in the wind, and now here was Blong.

What does a person say to a homesick Hmong kid who probably doesn't understand what's being said anyway? I didn't know.

Blong, waiting by the canoe racks, got a grip on himself, summoned up all his courage, and stepped toward me.

"Dave," he said, "Can you take me home?"

It was the longest sentence I had ever heard him speak.

I knelt down on the sand to be eye level with him and put my hand on his shoulder.

"Do you miss your mom and dad?" I asked.

He nodded and started to cry. It was the first time I had seen a Hmong boy cry. I patted him gently on the shoulder, and he cried all the more. Slowly we walked up toward the tents, my hand still on his shoulder. I did most of the talking. I asked him about his family, his brothers, and sisters. Then I talked about camp and the things we were going to be doing in the next few days, avoiding his original question. Blong made a supreme effort and got control of himself.

When we reached the tents, Blong's tent-line Chief, Dan Hess, was there. When Dan saw the two of us, he understood immediately what was happening. He took over for me, and I went down to the camp kitchen to get Blong some dinner. I knew he wouldn't want to face the other campers, given the state he was in.

The camp leaders held a council of war that night. I figured we had a maximum of twelve hours time to save Blong for camp, Scouting, and his own future growth and adjustment. I told the camp staff that as we decided what to do, there were two givens to keep in mind. First, this camp was not a prison. People could leave if they wanted to. Second, Blong was not going to leave. We had to figure out how to encourage him to stay.

As we talked, we realized that we weren't just dealing with Blong. We were dealing with many of our other Hmong Scouts too, perhaps all of them. It would have been nice to have had a Hmong consultant on our staff for advice, and, in time, we were to have many, but at that early date, we didn't have anyone. So we made our plans in the dark.

Early next morning I went to Chue Vue, who was a camper that year. I explained Blong's problem to Chue and told him why it was important that Blong stay in camp. Since Blong's parents didn't speak English, I asked if Chue would call them on the telephone and explain the situation, including my strong suggestion they urge Blong to stay at camp.

Chue made the call as I sat listening nearby. He spoke in Hmong, but now and then he would turn to me and report what was being said. I'd make a suggestion or two, and the conversation would continue. At last Chue turned to give his final report. The parents thanked us for calling and asked if we could bring Blong home when it was convenient for us.

"Tell them we'll do that," I said," but in the meantime we'll work on Blong and see if we can't get him to change his mind. Ask them if that's all right, and tell them we'll stay in touch by telephone."

It was all right. We still had a small margin of time.

Toward the end of breakfast in the Mess Hall, I stood up and called for quiet. I asked to see all the Hmong boys outside for a little meeting. Then I turned and walked out the door. Surprised and silent, but ever respectful, the Hmongs rose and followed me out. I led them down some wooden steps to the flats below the Mess Hall and had them sit down in a semi-circle under a butternut tree. They sat and looked at me, curious and expectant. Outwardly they were submissive, respectful Asians, but inwardly they dug their heels into the ground in stubborn resistance. Dan Hess was there; I had asked him to come for moral support. Blong was sitting in the front row of the circle.

I looked at them. The moment of truth had arrived, but I still didn't know what to say. I had to say something and it had to be good. It was my last chance.

"I know some of you have been thinking about going home," I said. "And it's all right to think that way sometimes. It means you have strong families, people who love you and wish the best for you. But I want you to know that I wish the best for you, too. Right now, the best thing for you is to stay at camp. This is where you learn independence, self-reliance, and how to get along by yourself away from home. You all came here to have fun, learn things, and make new friends, including American friends. If any of you gave up now and went home, it would be the wrong thing to do. It would make me very, very sad because I wouldn't want to lose you."

The sound of singing came drifting down from the Mess Hall. Breakfast was over, and the other campers were singing. I pointed up the hill.

"The American kids up there in the Mess Hall think about home, too. But they know they have to stay. They decided to come here to camp, and they're going to stick it out. They're going to make it. You can, too."

I looked around the circle. Their pre-literate, oral culture had made them used to eloquent talk. They could be swayed by it. But had they even understood me? They sat and looked at me, polite, attentive, unblinking. Suddenly I had an inspiration. I played all my cards.

"If you think you can stick it out, if you think you can stay, I want you to raise your hand," I said, and I raised my hand high in the air. Dan's hand went up, and one by one, some a little slowly, the Hmongs' hands went up. My new friends were giving me a tremendous vote of confidence.

I looked at Blong. His hand was up half-way.

Then Su Thao spoke up from the edge of the circle. His eyes twinkled and he grinned at me. He spoke in English so that I'd understand him. "Remember, guys," he said. "You're raising your hand. That means you've decided to stay."

It was over.

"You just made a wise, important decision," I said. "It will affect what happens to you for the rest of your life. I'm very glad for you. Now let's go and finish breakfast."

Later that day, the whole camp was out swimming, and I got a glimpse of Blong riding on Dan's shoulders. They were involved with a lot of others in some kind of rough horse-and-rider game. There was a lot of shouting, shoving, and splashing. Blong's face was wreathed in a beautiful smile.

How do you handle a Hmong kid who happens to be homesick? The same way you handle anyone else. You let him know that there is someone outside his immediate family who cares about him and wants the best for him.

That fall, Blong and his family moved to Duluth, and I didn't see him again for several years. However, he sent me a letter, which I quote here in full:

Dear Dave:

My name is Blong Xiong and I live in Duluth and I have fun play football and we win and we so happy that we win and we catch the fish and THE AND.

Pao Ly Vu

CHAPTER NINE

Pao Ly Vu

The poor are happy; the rich weep.

–Hmong saying

When I think of Pao Ly Vu, I think of a cold, slate-colored day and a muddy portage trail in Canada. I was wet and shivering after putting my canoe down in a lake at the far end of the portage. As I was returning over the trail looking for people who might need help, I heard a noise around the bend ahead of me. It was a loud, dissonant, whining sound. Was it a bear in agony or a moose trying to send a love signal? Then I realized it was someone singing. Down the trail came Pao, a huge pack on his back into which two of him could have fit with room to spare. He was plastered and caked in mud from his bare feet to his waist. His shoes were in one hand, a string of precious fish dragging along in the mud from the other. On his face was a grin as wide as a barn door.

When Pao saw me, he broke into a chant, "I like mud! Do you like mud? I like mud!" As he passed me he said, "There's some guys behind me who need help, Dave." Then he resumed his singing and disappeared along the path.

Pao Ly and his family came to Thailand in 1976, before the great influx of Hmong refugees. There were twenty people in the extended Vu family that crossed the Mekong River in fishing boats, including Pao's grandparents, aunts, uncles, and cousins. They spent their first night of freedom in a jail, where Pao remembers the food being very good. Then they moved into newly-built Camp Nongkhai, where there were buildings on cement slabs.

Each day, Pao put on the blue shorts, white shirt and long black stockings of a school boy and rode a bus out of camp to a Thai school. He could speak fluent Thai at the age of seven and understand Thai movies, though he was the youngest student in his class.

One day, there were no more buses leaving camp for school, and all the refugee boys went to work for Thai farmers. Pao earned money picking cucumbers. It was a long walk to the farm, but friendly Thais would often give him a ride in a pick-up. Eventually, Thai authorities closed the camp's gates, and Pao couldn't work any more.

Life in the camp was lots of fun for Pao and his buddies. They hunted birds with sling shots or set traps for them. But after a while the birds vanished. Fishing was also fun. Once Pao went to the Mekong River to fish. It was a long walk. While on that trip, some friendly Thais gave him octopus to eat, and it tasted good. Pao lost his two sisters to disease in Nongkhai, and a new little baby sister was born there.

In America, the Vus lived first in Oklahoma, because that was where their American sponsors lived. They were amazed by the enormous distances. People couldn't just run over to Dallas, Texas, to visit relatives.

Pao was enrolled in the third grade at an Oklahoma public school. He didn't know what was going on there. One time Pao was supposed to bring some cotton to school for a class experiment, but he didn't know what cotton was or where to get it. He was supposed to bring some celery to school another time and dip it in dye to show capillary action. But what in the world was celery? At school, Pao ate an apple for the first time. He was afraid of gym class and thought that the teacher would hit him with a ping-pong paddle if he couldn't do all the exercises.

In September, 1980, the Vus moved to Minneapolis. One day Pao was at the house of his friend Nhia Vang. Nhia had a Boy Scout handbook, and Pao asked what it was. This was his first exposure to scouting, and by 1984, the scouts of Troop 100 had elected Pao their Senior Patrol Leader. Bright, friendly and spunky, he proceeded to whip us into shape. We began winning contests and making our mark on the Hiawatha Scout District. We were the best show in town for about seventy Hmong boys.

Pao talks endlessly in Hmong with his buddies. When he laughs, he puts his whole body, soul, and stomach into the laugh. The veins in his neck nearly burst. One time I asked him if he was talking words or just babbling.

"Just babbling," he said.

At camp, Pao earned the nickname "Fun Guy," which was immediately corrupted into "Fungi." Riding in the middle of my canoe in Canada, he pointed at a loon flying by. "There go a Loony Bird!" he exclaimed. After that I called him and his paddling partner Chue Vue, the Loony Birds.

In the spring of 1986, Pao became one of the first five Hmong Eagle Scouts. For his Eagle project, he organized a presentation of the Hmong culture at Westminster Church, setting up a display of Hmong crafts in the Great Hall of the church. His mother came and discussed traditional Hmong embroidery, a craft that's already showing signs of dying out among the Hmongs in America. He got his friend Chue Vue to speak to the Westminster congregation during Sunday worship service. Chue spoke about problems the Hmong face in America. Pao then had some of the Scouts contribute their stories to a little booklet, "White as Rice, Clear as Water: Hmong Scout Stories," which he printed up for distribution. Thanks to Pao, a lot of Americans have learned a bit more about our new friends and neighbors.

Chue Hang

CHAPTER TEN

Chue Hang

Some day I wish to visit my country. Being a poor family here isn't happy, but we enjoy what we have. We're happy to be in America.

–*Chue Hang*, "White as Rice, Clear as Water"

Chue Hang was born in a small Hmong village near Long Cheng. The Hangs were farmers. Chue's father took care of the fish pools and rice fields, and hunted for food. Chue's mother cut grass for the horses and cows and fed them. Each year at New Year's time, all the different Hmong clans– Green, White and Black– got together to celebrate during three or four days of festivities. Everyone relaxed, had fun, and visited with friends. After that, with spring on its way, the Hmongs returned to work.

Chue's family moved around in Laos. Twice, they lived for a while in the city of Vientiane. They drove there in the back of a crowded Toyota pickup truck. But they moved back to farm once more in the vicinity of Long Cheng.

In 1976 the Hangs fled the country. Chue's older brother got them on a small fishing boat which took them across the Mekong River. They landed at Si Chang Mai across from Vientiane. For two months they lived in tents at a camp called Namphong. Then they moved to Ban Vinai.

The Hangs were among the first refugees at Ban Vinai. In fact, they helped build the camp. Originally, Ban Vinai and the hills around it were forested. This provided the refugees with construction material. While construction was taking place, they lived in tents, then moved into the buildings as they were completed. The Hangs lived in Ban Vinai for four years.

A fence surrounded Ban Vinai, but Chue ignored it. He spent most of his time wandering the fields and forests adjacent to the camp. He hunted, fished and swam in small streams. At night, he and his friends would build little huts of straw for shelter. When it was cold, they would huddle together for warmth. They got to know all the highways and byways of Ban Vinai, but kept to themselves to avoid trouble.

That was how Chue survived Ban Vinai. He lived by his wits in the forest, coming home to the camp now and then, but supporting himself with his hunting, fishing, and trapping.

Chue thinks he probably wouldn't have survived if he'd been solely dependent on camp fare. There never was enough, and it was unbearably bad. He would have weakened, become sick, and died, like so many others. Everyone in camp was left to survive on their own. Chue survived by living outside. Now and then he would bring home a string of birds or fish to supplement the family diet. His parents let him provide for himself because it was one less mouth to feed. Sometimes he'd help out by bringing home something particularly tasty. Chue hunted with a sling shot and Hmong cross bow. He also set traps, checking them each night and again in the morning. He remembers being stung by bees once while trying to get honey from a hollow tree.

There were about twenty friends who went adventuring with Chue at one time or another. Once they were shooting some mangoes down from a tree when one of his friends whispered that someone was coming. Terrified, Chue vaulted a fence and fled into the woods. From the safety of the brush, he watched a Thai farmer stroll by. When the coast was clear, the boys resumed their game. But they were always on the lookout.

The authorities eventually built a school in Ban Vinai that all the boys were expected to attend. Any child who could reach over his head and touch his left ear with his right hand was old enough to enroll. Chue could do this, but they had to catch him before he could be enrolled. In two months of school, he just couldn't conform. Every day they checked his fingernails, and every day his fingernails were uncut. He was hit regularly on the ends of his fingers with a ruler, but whatever lesson this was supposed to teach was lost to him. He finally quit and went back to the fields and forests. His family let him go.

Chue seldom played in the camp. Sometimes he and his friends carved wooden tops there. They would have wars in which one boy set his top spinning while the others tried to blast it off the field with their own. The boys found rubber bands and used them as currency for gambling. Chue had an eight foot string of them woven together. Toward the end of his stay in Ban Vinai, Chue got a job picking up litter in the market place.

It wasn't much fun for Chue inside camp. The wooded hills outside beckoned with the sound of birds singing from the trees. Creeks filled with fish ran everywhere. Outside the camp, Chue was on his own, completely free.

By 1979, however, the outside world began to change. Woods immediately surrounding the camp were slowly thinning, and Chue had to range farther afield in search of game. There were disturbing stories about the changing attitudes of Thai people. Hmongs caught outside the camp were sometimes beaten or killed, and Hmong women were being raped. This didn't stop Chue from leaving, but now he was more cautious and stayed closer to camp.

Chue's parents decided the time had come to apply for permission to emigrate to America. Chue wasn't particularly excited about leaving the camp, but he wasn't really sad, either. Many of his friends had already left. At last the day came when the Hangs boarded a bus for Bangkok.

Chue was amazed at all the traffic on the road. He had never seen so many cars and trucks. Every time the bus stopped, Thai farmers crowded around trying to sell the passengers roast chicken and fruit. Chue slept often during the trip.

In Bangkok, the Hangs stayed about two months at another refugee camp. The compound was a horrible place with nothing to do and nowhere to go. It was incredibly crowded, yet there were few people Chue could talk to. The camp food was awful. There were salty eggs Chue hated to eat. He often climbed up on a roof to watch the city with its jumble of cars, trains, and airplanes. He thought about the freedom he'd left behind in the hills around Ban Vinai and waited patiently. Eventually it was his turn to leave.

Chue and his family arrived in Honolulu, Hawaii, in mid-

1980. It was a perfect place, not too hot or cold, with a variety of fruits growing on the trees. Among the new friends Chue met there was a young Hmong boy named Yee Chang and his younger brother Chan. They had come to America shortly before Chue. The three boys explored the city by bus, fished in a park, and visited Waikiki Beach until Yee moved away to live with relatives in Minnesota.

The Hangs followed the Changs to Minnesota in December of 1981. Chue's dad was willing to work hard for a living, but it was difficult to find employment. He earned a little money cutting grass and washing dishes.

When Chue met Yee Chang in Minneapolis, Yee told him about a Boy Scout Troop he had joined. The Troop was meeting in a Salvation Army drop-in center at that time. This is where I met Chue. He became part of Yee's Patrol, and with Chan Chang, Xoua Pha, and Tou Lee, they were a winning patrol. At inter-troop camporees they would capture a good share of the ribbons. Whenever they went camping, Yee and Chue made sure their patrol had plenty to eat. Unlike many Hmong kids, they enjoyed preparing American meals. They learned to make pancakes and bake bread in a reflector oven. Meals were always feasts at their patrol campsite, featuring a combination of Hmong and American foods.

Xoua Pha

CHAPTER ELEVEN

Xoua Pha

One clump of bamboo, one trunk of the tree, one flesh and one skin.

–Hmong saying

In the fall of 1988, Xoua Pha called me on the telephone. I hadn't seen much of him since he graduated from Edison High School and went to work. It was good to hear his voice. He told me his father, mother, and the remainder of his family were arriving at the airport the following night from Thailand. It had been ten years since Xoua had seen them, and he asked me to be a part of the welcoming party at the airport.

By the time I arrived at the Minneapolis-St. Paul International Airport, a large crowd had gathered. Xoua was on the fringe of it, looking for me. He seemed tense and nervous. We conversed a little, catching up on events since last summer. Looking over the crowd, I noticed many Hmong families I knew. There were also many American friends and associates of the Hmong, some of whom I recognized. Floodlights from a local television station's camera bathed the gate door where passengers would emerge. Xoua and I continued talking at the edge of the crowd. He ignored the commotion around him, but periodically glanced over his shoulder in the direction of the gate.

Then in mid-phrase he glanced and turned pale as he saw his father.

"Excuse me, Dave," he said as he turned to me," I've got a

lot of tears saved up."

With that, Xoua dove into the crowd, pushing and elbowing his way toward the gate where a group of Asian travelers, looking tired and bewildered, were squinting in the floodlights' glare. I momentarily lost sight of Xoua, but by moving around and standing on tiptoe, I saw him throw himself into the arms of an older man. They held each other in a long embrace under the cameras. Then I lost my balance and my view.

People stepped aside to make way for the newcomers, and Xoua emerged, his eyes red, leading his father over to me. I made the Asian gesture of greeting with palms together. He responded in kind and we shook hands. With his father were his mother, a shy Hmong woman, and two brothers, one older, the other younger than Xoua. Awkward and lost, they had nothing to say. They answered my questions in monosyllables.

Xoua invited me to a party for the newcomers. Then the crowd surged past and went on its way.

Xoua Pha was born in a Hmong mountain village in Laos, the second youngest of six brothers. His family grew rice, corn, tobacco, and sugar cane. They also kept chickens, cows, and pigs. Their fields were about an hour's walk from the village over rugged terrain. Xoua went hunting with his older brothers and cousins when they'd let him. He was often left behind, however, because they thought him too small and noisy. When he came, they sometimes let him go around to a far point and drive the game toward them.

The family made pools for fish, and Xoua tried to catch them with his hands. Sometimes he succeeded. Xoua also had a fighting rooster that he took around the village, arranging fights with other boys' roosters. These rooster fights were exciting and broke up the routine of village life. People gathered around and made bets on which rooster would chase off the others.

One day the communists came to the village. They came suddenly, without warning, shooting and killing. There was no time to pack up and move out. Everyone just ran.

Xoua was still a little boy when he joined Troop 100. He was living with his older brother Xiong Pao. The rest of the family was back in Thailand.

Xoua grew up fast. After a few years in the Troop he was about my size, then perhaps just a little bigger. He was punchy.

If you shoved or punched him in fun, he punched right back. I liked to joke around with him about it.

"Xoua, you used to be a little wimpy guy," I would say. "What happened?"

"Now you're the wimp, Dave," was his reply.

Xoua was a student in my class. One day he entered my room wearing a large gold earring that I hadn't noticed before. I asked him to come over so I could have a look at it.

"It's none of your business," he grinned. "Just stay away."

"Relax, I just want to look at it," I persisted.

But he held one hand over the ear and waved me away with his free hand.

"Xoua, there's a law against a teacher punching a student, and I'm going to break it," I said. But I didn't. Nor did I ever get a close look at his earring.

Another time, when we were camping, Yee, Xoua, and I were doing some cooking over a fire. Suddenly the boys decided I needed a Hmong name. They talked a long time in Hmong, about what, I couldn't imagine. I just kept working over the fire while they talked. Then one of them informed me I was to be "Xeng Xou," which meant teacher or prophet or something like that.

When Xoua earned his Eagle Scout rank, there was the problem of who could stand up with him in place of his parents for the presentation ceremony. His older brother Xiong could serve as father, but what about a mother? Xoua asked his E.S.L. teacher Pat Budd to do it. She came to the ceremony and was his mother for the evening. Xoua presented her with a rose and a little silver Eagle pin to wear.

Su Thao

CHAPTER TWELVE

Su Thao

I had tooke 5 miles hike in the field around the Lac
(Calhoun) and Lake of Ielse at 1:30 to 6:00 p.m. I had picked
trash up in the trash can and swam for a while and fishing. I
got about ten crappies, but I threw them back. And I helped
a baby bird. It fell down from the nest. I had learned why
people like sunburn and take off their except the underwear
only and met a pretty girl. She told her name to me than I
told my name to her. So I had good time to hike with her.
She's about my size. Her age was 18.
  –*Su Thao*, "Su's Field Hike Around the Lakes", *6/30/82*

In 1986, some of our Hmong Scouts were starting to
think about what to do after high school. My friend Tom Hess
got the idea that we should establish a Hmong-American scholarship fund to help them out as they pursued their education.
Ten thousand Hmongs in the Twin Cities constituted one of the
largest refugee groups in the country. Being largely illiterate,
they were unemployable. Living in large extended families on
incomes of less than $10,000 per year, close to sixty percent of
them were dependent on public assistance. However, these
statistics may be improving slowly. The Hmong are bright, ambi-
tious, and hard-working. Dedicated to furthering their families'
fortunes, they possess many of the qualities Americans admire.

Yet the hope for a better future often fades when a Hmong
kid leaves high school. Government grants and loans and their

own summer employment fill only a part of the financial need. Grants don't take into consideration a Hmong student's need to live away from home. To try studying in the small, cramped quarters where many younger brothers, sisters, nieces and nephews get in the way and must be taken care of is often impossible. Grants don't consider a student's need to dress in normal American clothes rather than ill-fitting, second-hand cast-offs. Nor do grants cover expenses for important relaxation and entertainment. Students are already spending too many hours studying in order to keep up with their classmates who are having no trouble with the language.

As a result, Tom and a group of us formed a scholarship committee to raise money. We advertised for applicants and chose a candidate-selection committee to pick the winner. The selection committee picked Su Thao, one of our Scouts, to be the first recipient of the scholarship. He's now in his third year at Augsburg College in Minneapolis. Someday he hopes to have a job in the medical field and serve the Hmong people in one of their greatest areas of need.

Su Thao was born in March, 1968, in a large Hmong village in the Xiengkhouang province of Laos. Two clans were living there, the Thao and the Vang. They were separated by a river, which also bisected the village. The Thao lived on one bank, and the Vang on the other.

Su's father was a trader and businessman. He bought silver from the Hmong and sold it in nearby towns. He also had a large farm, where he planted the whole side of a hill with rice, corn, and vegetables. He raised pigs and chickens and regularly hunted wild animals.

Su's earliest memory is of going hunting with his father. They used a Hmong cross-bow. Su hunted by himself up in the mountains and set traps to catch squirrels and birds. One time, he stayed away too long and was punished when he returned.

The Hmong lived by tradition and considered themselves free from written laws, free to do the sensible thing and not worry about legalities. When a man once stole a pig from the Thaos, Su's father told him whatever he needed was his if he asked. That was all; the man wasn't punished.

There was a school in the village, and Su wanted to go to it, and wear the blue shorts and white shirt of a schoolboy. Somehow he and his friends got hold of a school math book.

They tore the pages out, and each boy got one to keep as his own personal textbook.

Su was excited on his first day of school, but after that he lost interest and wanted to quit. School was drudgery compared to the unlimited freedom he had known before. It was confusing and overwhelming. One day the teacher made him go to the front of the class and read from his notebook, but there wasn't anything in his notebook he understood. Su just stood there, tongue-tied and miserable. He would have quit school, but his parents wouldn't hear of it. Because he had made the decision to go to school, he'd have to stick it out. His parents dragged him there by the scruff of the neck.

Most days, Su rode a water buffalo to school. If he was late, he had to run around the school twice. He studied French, math, and writing under a strict teacher who knew everything there was to know about anything. During recess, students played running games, and those who didn't participate were given extra janitorial duties. Then the war came and interrupted Su's education.

Su had always known there was a war going on, but he didn't know anything about it. He could hear sounds in the distance, but didn't know who was fighting. Once he found some bazooka shells, and he and his friends played with them. They took them apart to get the gunpowder, poured it down a rat hole and lit it. The rats were demolished.

In 1975 the war moved closer, and people became fearful. The school was closed, children were told not to leave home or stray from the village, and men took turns standing watch all night. During the day, there was a superficial normality punctuated with whispered stories and rumors. Old horror stories about the Japanese occupation were heard once more. Only now, Vietnamese communists were the enemy, and everyone feared them. Airplanes flew overhead and the sound of bombing grew louder and closer. Su learned to live with the constant, gnawing burden of fear.

Su's father, Nhia Thao, decided the village was no longer safe for his family. His grandmother, however, refused to go. She said that if the sun set in Laos, it would rise where they were going. The family hesitated and made one false start, then moved out.

Since there were no roads, Su and his family walked the

trails on foot. Everyone carried a share of the burden. Su carried some extra clothing; his dad carried his three small brothers, Xay, Xia and Blong, and Su's sister walked. Half the village went with them. They walked from early morning to sunset. Su had never been so far from home. He saw abandoned belongings on the trail from the many people who had passed that way before them. Now some of the group began sitting down and dropping out; others turned back. Near the end of the day they reached a fast-flowing river that was too large to wade across. Utilizing a rope strung from the opposite side, one of Su's relatives did what Westerners might call a Tyrolean traverse. He crossed the river by pulling himself, hand over hand, along the rope and brought a boat back.

About a hundred people spent the night on the other side of the river. Since Su's father was a prominent man in the community, his family was permitted to stay in a little hut. The following day they reached a major highway. From there, a truck took them on a six-hour ride to a town close to Vientiane, where they stayed with a missionary Catholic priest for two days.

A communist regime had taken over the country and its grip was tightening everywhere. There were too many refugees on the roads, and the government didn't want them moving about. People were soon prohibited from traveling without written permission.

During the New Year's celebration, Nhia told the mayor of the town that he was taking his family to Vientiane to celebrate. The mayor gave him passes for two families.

Nhia hired a pick-up truck and driver, and, late one evening, two families packed themselves and all their remaining belongings into it and headed south toward Vientiane. They passed several check-points. Each time, at the black-and-white control gates, communist Pathet Lao soldiers looked at their passes and swung the gates open. At first their going was smooth. Then, at the last check-point, they ran into trouble. The guard wouldn't open the gate for them. Their pick-up was allowed to pass, but the passengers had to get out. Nhia led his family on foot as they detoured around the check-point. Beyond it, he hailed another pick-up, and they were bound for Vientiane once again.

Living in Vientiane was an important Hmong leader who owned a large house. Nhia and his family made for the refuge of that house. When they arrived, it was crowded with refugee families, and the gate to the compound was shut and locked. There was no room for two more families. Regardless, noticing a tiny space under the gate, and with no one around, Nhia squeezed his children, one by one, into the compound.

Now the children were in, but their parents were outside. Su was sick with fear for his parents and wondered if he'd ever see them again. Eventually, however, they too got in.

The house was packed with refugees trying to avoid being seen from the street. The children were instructed not to run across the driveway, which was visible from the street. If you were on one side, you stayed there no matter what.

Next door to the Hmong house where they were hiding was a Lao house with chickens in the yard. The Thao boys laid a trail of corn kernels which some of the chickens followed into an ambush. Now they had chicken to eat.

Most of the families in the house were at the end of their material, mental, and spiritual resources. They sat there helplessly. But Su's father was resourceful, courageous, and never quitting. He disappeared into downtown Vientiane on business. While Su waited in agony and suspense, Nhia took silver to town to trade for cash. He made some deals and arranged for his family to be rescued by boat and carried to Thailand.

The family would split up for the passage. Su's mother, Khoua Yang, and the three little boys would go first, disguised as a Lao fishing family. The effort flopped badly because the boys wouldn't stop crying, and none of them looked like fisherfolk. It was too risky. Their Lao guide called the whole thing off and sent them back to the Hmong house.

Nhia tried again the next day. This time his children had exchanged their Chinese-Hmong trousers for ragged Lao clothes. Su and his sister were to go first with a Lao man and woman. Before Nhia turned his children over to these strangers, he paid. But in paying, Nhia tore the money in two and gave them only half, saying to the man, "When you bring me proof that my children are safe, you will get the rest of the money."

Su carried a note addressed to a relative who was already in Thailand. The stranger was to carry the signed note back to Nhia. Su and his sister also carried money in a pocket sewn into their sashes.

The woman to whom Su and his sister had been entrusted took them to a house to wait. At the house, she noticed that the children were carrying money. When she started to take the money from Su's sister, Su tried to grab it from her hand, and there was a scuffle. The money was torn. Now the two children were at the mercy of a couple they didn't trust. Their parents were gone, and they had no one to turn to. Su was sure something terrible would happen.

Nevertheless, the Lao woman must have had a good heart. Or maybe she knew she'd eventually get more money by playing Nhia's game, for she faithfully carried out her end of the bargain.

The woman took them to the river, where they boarded a small canoe. The trip across was long and slow, a journey from darkness into light. On the way, Su thought, "I'm making it." When he got to the other side, his first feeling was the thrill of simply being alive.

The Lao woman took them to Camp Nongkhai, where Su's maternal grandparents were already waiting. One of the first people Su saw there was his mother's cousin. The cousin looked at the two children, laughed and, pretending to scold them, asked if they had run away from home.

After Su and his sister, Xay crossed alone. When he reached Thailand, he was put in a hut with another young Hmong child. He stayed there most of the day, and, later in the afternoon, he was taken up to a road to wait for a bus. When a bus came along, Xay got aboard. Inside were his mother and two youngest brothers.

By the time they reached the camp, it was dark. They were all together again except for their father Nhia. Would he make it? They waited and called in a shaman, but the shaman couldn't tell them what had happened to their father. The night passed.

Meanwhile, Nhia was arranging his own escape. He didn't want to come totally impoverished to Thailand. Instead, he was doing some silver-trading. He acted as a middleman between Hmong and Lao, picking up some survival money. During his last transaction, a Lao man held out money to him and asked if he wanted to count it. Suddenly Nhia realized the man intended to kill him as he counted, so he grabbed the money and ran. He headed for Thailand and arrived in Nongkhai one day after his family.

The Thaos stayed in Camp Nongkhai for six months. Conditions there were intolerable. They lived in a three-sided box with one end open. There was no privacy.

Every day, Su's mom, Khoua Yang, could hear drums beating for the dead. Each day they seemed closer, and she was sure her family's turn was coming. But Nhia Thao had a dream. In the dream he had a bunch of bananas. A Lao man wanted to buy them, but Nhia covered the bananas with a piece of cloth and wouldn't sell them. He knew what the dream meant. The bananas were his children, and by covering them with cloth, he had saved them from death by disease. The beating drums came no closer.

Nhia tried to get his family out of Nongkhai and into the Hmong camp at Ban Vinai, but he couldn't get permission to leave. Finally, he made a deal with a driver who delivered food to the camp. The driver hid the family under some boxes in the back of his pick-up and put Nhia in the cab. When they stopped at the camp gate, Nhia explained that he was going into town for some supplies. The excuse wasn't good enough; they were turned back. Later, they tried another gate, and this time they made it. After six months, they were finally out of Nongkhai.

Now the challenge was to get into Ban Vinai. First, Nhia had to obtain permission to pass through several military checkpoints on the road from Nongkhai to Pakchom, a little town on the Mekong River near Ban Vinai. Somehow, he gained permission through friends in Nongkhai, so they drove the pick-up truck along the winding river road to Pakchom. They drove for most of the day with the river on their right, and the dark, brooding hills of Laos beyond. The Hmong people have a saying, "*Ntuj tsaus, av tsaus*," which means "Dark sky, dark land." Su watched the darkening hills of his homeland and wondered if he could ever leave that darkness completely behind.

At Pakchom, the Thaos bought their way into Ban Vinai using contacts through relatives with the Thai government. It took almost all their remaining money, but Nhia was able to purchase two I.D. cards for Ban Vinai, which entitled the family to food rations for two of its members. Since it was as good as they could get, it would have to do. In this way the Thaos became illegal residents of Ban Vinai. But no one bothered with legalities.

The Thaos lived for a while with Su's maternal grandmother, of the Yang clan, who was already a resident of the camp. Then they built their own place in the Thao quarter.

The family's fortunes began to improve when Nhia was elected leader of a section of the camp. They had their own water tank, so the boys didn't have to line up and wait four or five hours. They received more supplies, even ice. Su and his brothers had never seen ice before. They didn't know what to do with it and tried frying it in a pan. As leader, Nhia could have moved his family into a fancy house with electricity. Not wanting to move away from his Thao relatives, however, he stayed where he was.

The boys had fun in Ban Vinai. There was a lake where they fished with nets and went swimming. They also hunted for meat in the uplands because rats feeding on upland rice were more tasty than the camp fare. They caught chameleons and tried to make pets of them. There were large bugs with rhinoceros-like horns that could be trained to fight each other, and almost every boy in Ban Vinai had a fighting rooster. They would bring their roosters around looking for a match. When a fight started, everyone would gather around to watch. Tops were favorites, and every kid had a top made for him by his father or a favorite uncle. A crowd of boys would gather to spin them and choose up sides for regular top wars. When one top knocked over another or blasted someone else's to bits, it gave the winner a sense of mastery. But a boy's most valuable possession was his slingshot. With it, he could wander around camp all day, shooting everything that moved except people.

School was free in Ban Vinai, so lots of children attended. Many skipped classes, but Nhia paid to send Su to special English classes that were held one hour before school. There were final tests for which the top three students were given prizes. Su collected a box full of books and colored pencils as prizes for top achievement in school.

Su and his brothers discovered the American volunteer workers at Ban Vinai and ran after them like everyone else. One of the Americans had a tiny little daughter who, with her blue eyes and blond hair, looked like a little china doll. Su couldn't believe she was real. He ran after her, watching in amazement as she toddled around.

Su got sick at Ban Vinai, so sick that everyone thought he was dying. The Thaos did not know what kind of disease he had, and not even a shaman could help. Su was out of his head with fever. His father paid money to get him into the hospital in Loei and stayed there with him while Su recovered.

Su's illness was a turning point for his father. Nhia decided he couldn't stay there at the risk of his family's health. He would have to get them to America if possible.

There were terrible stories circulating about families being split up in America, and people being fed to monsters. But the Thaos discounted them as rumors. What of the horrible jumble of garbled nonsense that they saw on television, though?

In spite of his reservations, Nhia applied for refugee processing. When he explained at the interview that he'd been a soldier working for the American C.I.A., the family was on its way to America.

Su Thao and his family arrived at the Minneapolis-St. Paul International Airport in the dead of a cold winter night. Walking off the ramp and into the waiting room, Su felt the cold indifference of a thousand strange faces. Although he had studied some English, the conversation around him was utterly incomprehensible. Then Su saw his relatives, his Yang grandparents, his mother's brothers and sisters and others. Su knew them all. Suddenly he felt a new life had just begun.

The Thaos picked up their baggage and stepped outside to face the full sub-zero blast of winter. The physical and psychological shock was profound. With only sandals on his feet, Su could hardly walk. But he stumbled along with his bundle, following the others. Would they walk all night?

They stopped in the parking lot by a row of cars belonging to the Yangs. Su's uncle motioned him into one. In his excitement, Su forgot his freezing feet and climbed in, wondering when his father would own a car like his uncle's.

They drove off into the night through a labyrinth of brightly-lit freeways and whizzing cars. At last they stopped in front of the home of the Thaos' American sponsors. Members of Su's family emerged from the other cars. They walked up to the door and rang the bell. Su's feet were freezing by now, and he was in agony from the pain. But he made no complaints. Soon a boy and girl a little older than Su answered the door.

As the Thaos walked into the house, a large, terrifying dog barked at them, but someone spoke to the dog and it lay down. To the Americans' friendly words and gestures, Su just smiled. The Yang relatives stayed a few minutes, then left.

The woman of the house took Su's smallest brothers upstairs and Su followed. She took them to a room with a bright light and a large tank of water. She talked baby-talk to them in a kindly way, trying to get them to do something. They didn't understand what she wanted, so they just stared at the water.

Su took a guess and told his brothers to take off their clothes and get into the water. He was right. The woman gave them soap and shampoo and showed them how to wash. When they were finished, she dried them with a towel and gave them some strange, loose-fitting clothes to put on.

Su went downstairs and told the others what he had seen, so they figured this was what they were also supposed to do. After his bath, Su and his brothers were shown to a bedroom. There was a television set the boys wanted to watch, but Su didn't know how to get it started. Instead, they just went to bed.

Next morning, still wearing the strange, loose-fitting clothes, Su went downstairs to the kitchen. The woman was showing Su's mother how to use an electric stove. It was a strange thing that didn't use wood or make flames, and there was a little clock on it. Su's mother made breakfast. When it was ready, she called everyone to come and eat, including the sponsors. They sat in a bright, sunny room and ate breakfast. But the sponsors didn't eat with the Thaos. Su drank some soda pop and had a little fruit. That was all. He wore his pajamas all day.

The Thaos lived with their sponsors for a week until Nhia decided to move the family out. It was just too hard for his large family to try to live in another family's house. He didn't know how to use a telephone, but gave his brother-in-law's number to the sponsor and got through to Su's uncle. The uncle explained to the sponsors that the Thaos needed their own house, and eventually their sponsors found one.

Su Thao was one of the charter members of our Hmong Boy Scout Troop. To me, at first, he was just a nice Hmong kid, a little shy and self-conscious, but friendly — hardly distinguishable from the others. Slowly, however, I came to appreciate the enormous reserve of character that had sustained Su on his long journey.

We were camping one winter night at Camp Ajawah, thirty or forty of us sleeping on bunks in the camp lodge, when I was jolted awake by a terrible crash. I sat up and opened my eyes in utter darkness. The fire had gone out, and the room was icy cold. There was no sound other than the even breathing of the sleeping boys. Yet I knew that someone had fallen out of an upper bunk and was lying on the floor. I groped for the light switch in bitter cold and turned it on, but the flood of light failed to wake anyone.

On the floor next to one of the beds I saw a heaped-up sleeping bag. I bolted over to it, and Su got there just as I reached the victim. Shivering in his underwear, his breath steaming in the frosty air, Su knelt down and drew open the sleeping bag. Yu Pheng Vu lay there, his eyes wide open, with a frightened look. Su spoke to him reassuringly in Hmong, felt his limbs and had him sit up slowly.

"He's all right," Su whispered. "He was dreaming about ghosts."

We helped Yu Pheng into bed, and Su returned to his own bed. I turned off the lights, crawled into my sleeping bag and lay there thinking in the darkness. Why had Su, of all that crowd, been the one to get up out of his warm bed and come to the rescue? There was no particular reason for him to get up, but he did it anyway, as a matter of course. He had made it his responsibility, though he didn't have to. And he handled the situation well, with just the right touch. I felt I'd learned a little more about Su Thao that night.

One day Dan Hess and I got into a discussion with Su and some other Hmong Scouts. I asked them if they thought it was important to have a Hmong Scout Troop; why not just join up with a mainstream Troop?

"Because the Hmong Troop brings a new challenge to other Troops and helps them improve," said Su.

"I learned about the Hmong culture in Troop 100," added Yu Pheng. "We make Hmong tops and pop guns and play Hmong games. I never knew how to do those things until I joined Scouts."

"If it wasn't for Scouts, I'd just sit home and wouldn't know anything," said Chan. "Life would be tougher if there wasn't Boy Scouts."

"OK," said Dan, "but why a Hmong Troop?" Couldn't they do all those things as part of a mainstream Troop?

"The Hmong Troop is important to the Hmong community," said Yee. "It gives families a chance to see what their children have learned in America. It says to everyone, Hmongs can accomplish something in America as Hmongs."

"We feel great about ourselves because we're part of a group that can overcome obstacles," said Su. "We get the confidence to meet new challenges."

"OK, I wanted to know how you felt. If you want a Hmong Troop, so do I," I said.

"Are you sure, Dave?" asked Xay Thao, Su's younger brother.

Yes, I was sure.

Later that year at the Hmong New Year celebration in the Minneapolis Auditorium, Troop 100 marched onto the stage and built a twenty-foot signal tower in a few minutes, using ropes and poles. When it was finished, Chan Chang scrambled to the top of it, and signaled "Happy New Year" to the assembled Hmong community in semaphore code.

In 1985, Su Thao and Chue Vue were chosen to take part in the Boy Scout World Jamboree in Calgary, Canada. Before they left, I told them, "You're Americans now, just like any native born American. You'll be representing America and everyone you meet will think of you as Americans, as Yanks. You're Hmong, too, of course, and you'll represent Hmong people. That's also something to be very proud of."

That same year, the Scouts of Troop 100 elected Su Thao their Senior Patrol Leader. He won the Good Scout Cup in 1985, and in 1986 he became the first Hmong Eagle Scout. In that same year, I hired him to be Chief of the junior camp at Ajawah. When I called him up on the telephone and asked him to take the job, there was a long pause, and then he asked if I was kidding. No, I wasn't kidding. I had seen Su in action. I knew he could do it.

I presented Su with the Camp Director's Award in the summer of 1983 when he was still just a fledgling camper. But I saw then that he had enormous potential and I wanted to point it out to others by giving him the award. In the citation, paraphrasing the Scout Law, I called him "trustworthy, loyal, brave, a friend to all and a brother to every camper." In the coming years, he was to vindicate my early confidence in him.

Chue Vue

CHAPTER THIRTEEN

Chue Vue

I want to see my family tree. I want to see my children, my wife, my brothers and friends. I want to see their smiling faces again. I am a slave, a porter for the enemy, hungry and poor. How can I live like this for ten or twenty more years? I want to be free.

—Wang Vue, uncle of Chue Vue in a tape smuggled out of Laos, 1987.

Chue Vue was born in Samthong, the Hmong stronghold near the Plain of Jars, in 1969. The family home was in Hua Sa Tou, several days away from Samthong by footpath. That's where Chue's earliest memories begin. As a small boy, he brought food and water to the fields where his family raised rice, corn, and cucumbers. As the youngest boy, Chue was destined to be a farmer all his life. His older brothers would go to school and advance the family fortunes with their knowledge. Chue would work the soil. He bitterly resented this. He wanted to put on the blue shorts and white T-shirt that were the uniform of the schoolboy. It seemed that all the village boys except Chue went to school. He cried and cried, but his job was to watch the animals. Finally, Chue's uncle convinced his father to let him go.

Chue was a schoolboy for half a year, until his village was engulfed by war. About fifty boys and girls attended the school. The teacher was an eighteen-year-old Lao boy. He was very nice and very intelligent, but he was tough. He was the only Lao in the little Hmong village. Chue considered him an excellent teacher, but when the war came to that part of Laos, he left.

Chue's mother died in 1974. She hadn't been well for a long time. She felt tired and dizzy and became weak. Eventually she was unable to walk, and lay in bed for two days. When she seemed a little better, she rose and went into the fields. Chue went with her. She told Chue to bring her a bucket of water, and with these words, she suddenly became dizzy, collapsed and died.

Chue's mother had always considered his oldest brother to be her favorite son. He was number one in his class in school, a very good student who excelled in debate and math. But Chue's mother, in death, wanted her favorite son with her; the boy grew weak, became sick and died three or four months after his mother's death. Now her son was with her at last.

A year later, Chue's father died. After the death of his wife, he had gone to Vientiane on business, leaving Chue, his brothers, and sisters in the care of his grandmother. Chue's father was part farmer, part merchant, and also worked for the American C.I.A. Chue never knew precisely why or how his father died in Vientiane, but heard that he had been poisoned.

War had been a part of Chue's life from the beginning, even though he understood little of what was going on. There were distant explosions and reports of fighting, and his father and uncles were involved. His uncles were soldiers, and in 1967, before Chue was born, his father had been drafted into the Royal Lao Army, but had been deferred as head of the family.

Chue's family moved frequently in his early years. Once they were evacuated by helicopter to Phak Khe, where they lived for two years. Then they returned by foot to Hua Sa Tou. There must have been a great battle near Hua Sa Tou, for dead soldiers lay everywhere. While the villagers set about burying them, Chue went with his grandfather to retrieve supplies that had been hidden in caves before they left.

In 1975, Hua Sa Tou was bombed. It was daytime and most of the people were away in the fields. Chue was at home with the old people and small children. He heard the sound of airplanes as they appeared overhead. They began dropping bombs, and people ran and hid. Chue crawled under a fallen tree. Explosions were everywhere, and one bomb burst about fifty feet from Chue.

After a long time, the airplanes left. There was an aftermath of great destruction. Buildings were leveled or burning. Injured people were crying out. Many had died.

For some, the village was no longer safe or livable. The villagers moved to the forest and made shelters from boughs. They didn't establish a permanent settlement because they were afraid it would be spotted and bombed. They tended their fields from this forest hide-out.

Back in the village, four communist soldiers arrived. They were the Pathet Lao, or Red Lao. They told the villagers that the war was over, looked around and left. A few days later, they returned, but didn't stay. Then they came a third time, asking questions and writing down answers. How many people lived here? How many chickens, pigs, and cows were there? Much of this wealth would have to be taken and shared with the new rulers. Who was doing the work? Who had fought on the side of General Vang Pao, the Hmong chief? All loyalists would have to join the communist forces now.

The new rulers called a meeting in the village. They began to teach communism at the meeting. Some young men of the village kept hidden, but others attended these meetings and joined the communists. They were taken away to be soldiers. Chue never saw them again. One of the "volunteers" was Chue's uncle, Wang Vue. Chue had no word of this uncle until 1987.

Since all the men had either fled, died, hidden, or been sent away by the communists, Chue's aunt was chosen by the new rulers to be village leader. She was a large woman, physically formidable, a natural leader. Anyone could see this. But she was not about to do the bidding of the communists. One night she took Chue, his brother, sisters, and grandmother and went to join the men hiding in the forest. Chue slept under a full moon that night in an open field of rice seedlings. It was a perfect night, warm and still.

Chue lived in the forest for three years, running and hiding. Sometimes it could be very peaceful in the woods. Chue would wake up early and hear birds singing and squirrels chattering. His grandmother would tell him to go and pick mushrooms. He caught fish in small creeks and searched for crabs and crayfish. He would come home each evening and give his grandmother the food he'd collected that day. Sometimes they were able to harvest cucumbers and pumpkins. They would eat the pumpkin leaves. Once in a while, one of his uncles would bring back some meat.

During that time, Chue saw much fighting, many people hurt or killed, and lots of first aid and medicine being administered. Other people slowly joined the group he was with until there were more than five hundred of them constantly moving and fighting. They supported and were protected by a group of guerrillas who called themselves Chao Fa. They lived mostly in the vicinity of Mount Phu Bia, where bombing was constant, around the clock. It became impossible to sleep at night, and during the day, Chue watched from hiding as trees were blown apart and rocks were shattered by the bombing.

The climactic struggle with the communists came in 1977 in a two-day, two-night battle on Mount Phu Bia. Chue was camped with his family two miles from the fighting. He could hear shooting and voices crying out. Chue carried cooked rice to the soldiers. He saw men shooting and others lying wounded and dying. A few yards away lay wounded communist soldiers, calling for help.

While carrying rice for the soldiers, Chue's sister was hit by a fragment. She received superficial wounds which covered her with blood. She began screaming because she thought she was going to die.

As the battle crept closer, Chue's uncle decided to evacuate the family. The Chao Fa wanted him to stay and fight, but he told them he had to save his family.

There was no food. People were starving, and the soldiers were hungry too. Chue's uncle decided to kill his cow, give the meat to the soldiers and go.

Under airplane attack the next day, Chue, two uncles, two aunts, a cousin, and his grandfather's two wives, one of whom was Chue's grandmother, fled the fighting. The grandfather's other wife, Chue's step-grandmother, was a very old woman. She was blind, so the men took turns carrying her. But it soon became clear that this wouldn't work. She would slow them down so that none would escape. They found a well-concealed cave for the old woman, left some food and opium, said goodbye, and ran.

The Vues ran for one day, never stopping to look back. They were coming down from Mount Phu Bia and circling it at the same time to keep the mountain between them and the fighting. They found some rice and chickens in a deserted village, but there was no time to kill and cook a chicken. Their flight continued.

They fled in this way for several days. The villages they passed were mostly empty, but they could rest in them. At last they came to a small, nearly empty town where they felt relatively safe. They had nothing; no more rice or salt, only a little corn and some potatoes. They started to build a house.

They thought about the blind old grandmother they'd left behind to die. It had been a terrible thing to do, a violation of their most sacred values. Yet it was a matter of survival. They wondered if she was dead. Perhaps they should send someone back to check on her. With any luck, the communists might not have reached the cave where they left her.

A search party consisting of Chue's uncle and some young men from the village was sent back to find the old woman. They found the grandmother still alive in the cave. She had eaten the food and taken the opium, but it had not been enough to kill her.

Two men began carrying the old woman, but they were surprised by a communist patrol. In the firefight that followed, one young man was killed, but the others, including Chue's step-grandmother, got away. They never retrieved the body of the young man who was killed. He had just married.

Chue's family stayed in their new village for two weeks. During this time, the communists moved closer. Chue could hear the sound of guns. It was time they discussed a course of action to take. If they returned to surrender, there was no telling what might happen. Escaping to Thailand was their only option, but Chue's grandmother wouldn't leave her country for a foreign land.

"We have to go," said Chue's sixteen year old sister. "Your son's life is in danger; we're going. If you stay, you stay by yourself."

The Vues didn't want to leave their grandmother to die, so they picked her up and forced her to walk. However, the blind old step-grandmother who had just been rescued had to be left a second time. This time they left her a lot of opium and told her to die.

The Vues were part of a group of about one hundred people walking to Thailand. They walked for a month. It was spring, and rice and corn were beginning to grow. The land lay fresh, green, and beautiful where they walked.

They came to a small town occupied by several families. The residents were very poor and had no animals, food or money. One man was very sick. He had a daughter ten or twelve years of age that he wanted to sell. Chue's sister needed a companion, and the little girl might be a nice wife for one of the boys some day. The Vues, however, had no money, so the man sold his daughter to someone else, and the Vues kept going.

Chue's uncle had a German Shepherd dog that they tried several times to leave, but it stayed with them. One night, the group camped by a small, swift-flowing river. They worried about how to cross it, for people had drowned in rivers like this. Suddenly the dog appeared and ran around, excited but not barking. Was he trying to tell them something? He plunged into the bushes, and Chue's uncle followed. The dog led him to a path. Not far along it, the uncle discovered a small settlement. From the safety of some bushes, he observed a car and some communist soldiers.

The uncle hurried back to warn the others. They would have to cross the river tonight, or they'd be discovered and killed the next morning. There was no time to lose.

Women were told to keep their children quiet at all costs. If a child should cry, they would all be killed. But the children were exhausted and slept.

Secretly and quietly, the Vues began building a raft. They cut bamboo and lashed it together to make a three-person platform. Then they strung a rope across the river. It took all night to get everyone to the other side, but by morning they had all made it except one tiny baby who woke up crying. His parents fed him opium, and he died.

First light found the refugees on the other side, exhausted and hungry. Yet they had to get farther away. Some people sat down to eat rice, while others began climbing a steep, uphill path. They felt safer as they climbed, and some began talking in low voices. Soon everyone was talking.

Chue was walking with his uncle about half-way up the hill when the sound of rocket-fire began. Chue's uncle cried, "Down!", and Chue hit the ground just as a shell tore into the people behind him. A girl who had been walking ten feet from him had half her leg torn away.

Chue and the others got up and ran. They reached the top of the hill, panting, their throats dry. Chue's uncle passed a bucket of water around.

As soon as they had set up camp on the other side of the hill, their scouts returned with word that the communists were crossing the river. Everyone began running. They kept moving for six days and six nights. All the while, Chue ran bare-footed, and a bleeding cut on his big toe became infected and swollen. He could hardly walk, but he had to keep going. No one could carry him if he stopped.

Chue almost got lost at one point. They were crossing an open area in the neighborhood of Samthong, now a communist stronghold. The grass had grown so tall that Chue couldn't see over it. Pathways criss-crossed in every direction, and Chue, his sister, and grandmother were very tired and falling behind. Chue had to fight to keep himself from falling asleep. They had to get through the grass and past Samthong before sunup.

Suddenly, Chue fell. In the darkness, he had stumbled into a huge hole. He pitched forward, grabbed hold of a root, and hung there. His grandmother was walking just ahead of him and heard the jostle of the cook-pots he was carrying on his back. She turned, searched around and found him in the darkness. Taking his arm, she pulled him to safety. Chue never knew how deep the hole was or what was at the bottom.

As they caught up with the others, they could hear a baby crying. People told the mother to do something. At first she refused, but finally she fed it opium.

Then more babies began crying. Suddenly, gunfire shattered the stillness, and people scattered. Children were screaming. Old people were left behind. Chue held tight to his grandmother's hand as they ran. When they stopped, the grandmother sat down and said she could not go any farther.

Chue's uncle seemed to agree. Her age was keeping them back. Chue, holding his grandmother's hand, remembered what had happened to his blind step-grandmother.

"We can't leave you here," said Chue's sister. "If you die here, we can't bury you."

"Leave me," said the grandmother, "and leave your little sister to stay with me."

There was no way they would do that. So once again they

forced the old woman to keep going.

The group was now headed for Thailand. One of the men had a compass, and directed them south. Since there was very little food, they ate leaves and wild potatoes. They met people coming back from the Thai border who had not made it across because of the many communist soldiers there. In the forest they encountered a group of friendly young men who turned out to be communist soldiers. One of them was a Hmong who had lost his family in an escape attempt. Now he was forced to serve the communists.

One day firing broke out in front of them. Dashing up a hill to escape, Chue dropped a pack sack containing ten pounds rice. Safe at the top, his family scolded him, saying that now he would have to go hungry.

There was a steep trail down the other side of the hill. Chue's brother, weak and tired, slipped and went tumbling down. They thought he was hurt, but when Chue reached him, he sat up and said he was all right.

Proceeding cautiously, the Vues passed around a mine planted under a tree placed across the path. Suddenly there was shooting. Chue turned around and bumped into his uncle, knocking him down. Chue, his uncle, and his uncle's little daughter all fell down together as bullets whizzed overhead and thudded into trees. When they got up and ran, Chue dropped another pack.

Now the refugees were scattered all about the forest. The Vues crossed a creek and sat down beside a steep hill. There they discovered Chue's aunt was missing. Darkness brought torrential rains. The Vues lay on wet leaves and tried to sleep. When the rain abated, Chue heard an animal, perhaps a tiger, whining. He slept very little.

In the morning they found the path, and the group slowly gathered itself together again. Chue's aunt appeared, along with many other people. A few men were left behind to cover their flight. At the top of a hill, one man climbed a tree. In the distance, he saw the city of Vientiane and the Mekong River.

Some people there had already failed to cross the river twice because of all the soldiers. They warned the others to avoid the heavily guarded bridge. A whole family had been wiped out trying to get under it.

Some people were for turning back, while others wanted

to attempt the river acrossing. After holding a conference, they decided to split up into small groups. The babies would be given opium to make them sleep.

At midnight, Chue's group of three families set out. After a while, they came to a small river which would take them to the Mekong if they found a boat. Children and women hid in some bushes while the men scouted about. They returned with two boats. The boats didn't have enough space for three families, so one had to turn back. Since the three families were closely related, it was a very difficult parting. Chue's uncle gave his gun and two bullets to the family staying behind. They wished each other the best of luck, and the head of the family being left behind urged the others to "come back and save us if you can." Chue's boat almost sank under the weight of the nine people in his family. Chue was placed up front to watch for rocks. He could hear fish jumping in the gurgling water, but could see nothing in the blackness.

The river twisted and turned. As they paddled along, Chue strained his eyes, but could see nothing. He was soon aware of the dark bulk of a bridge. They stopped paddling and drifted noiselessly. Chue could hear soldiers walking on the bridge as they slipped quietly beneath it. No one moved. No one breathed. They drifted out at last into a broad, black stretch of water. They were on the Mekong. Further and further they drifted. Chue's uncle was paddling carefully now. The pale light of dawn lit the sky. Ahead lay the black shape of Thailand. They began whispering, then talking. Chue's uncles were both churning the water furiously with their paddles.

Rifle fire erupted from the direction of the bridge as they were spotted in the growing light, but they were already out of range, and the canoe ground up safely on the sandy Thai shore.

One of the first people Chue met in Thailand was a young Hmong man who had come under the bridge with his family three or four days before. They had been swimming in the water, clinging to bamboo. The guards on the bridge had spotted them and begun shooting. His father, mother, wife and brother were all killed. He had escaped by hiding among rocks on the shore. He saw them capture his son and drag the boy away. Now he was all alone.

Chue stayed for a year in the refugee camps of Thailand; first Nongkhai, then Ban Vinai. He found life hard there. The camps were overcrowded, and the stink of garbage and overflowing toilets was everywhere. No one could leave the camp without special permission, and food was scarce. They were fed only two meals a day. Many people died of disease. Chue's family raised vegetables which they sold to the Thais, and Chue received a little education. He learned to read and write Thai.

Since Chue's uncle had been a soldier, the family's name eventually appeared on the list of those accepted for admission to America. As a result, they were moved to Bangkok, where they stayed three months while being processed. Then they were flown to America.

Chue was tremendously excited when he landed in Hong Kong. He thought it was America until someone told him otherwise. When he finally did step off the plane in America, barefooted and wide-eyed, Chue was amazed at what he saw — cars, tall buildings, strange-looking people. He had seen his first American in Nongkhai. Now the world seemed full of them, each one strange and different. It was amazing to him. Yet there was freedom here, and you could come and go as you pleased.

Chue lived in Philadelphia for a year. There were nine in his family — Chue, his brother Chong, his two sisters, his aunt and uncle and their two tiny children, and his old grandmother, who had endured so much.

Chue started school in America thinking it would be like those in Thailand. To his surprise, there were no uniforms. You didn't have to stand up and greet the teacher, and most puzzling of all, you didn't have to pay attention to the teacher. In fact, some of the pupils didn't listen to the teacher at all. Others argued back with impunity. They fooled around and weren't punished. Chue was horrified by this. He couldn't understand a word of what was going on.

In the cold January of 1981, Chue and his family moved to Minneapolis, where he soon joined our Hmong Boy Scout Troop. Later that spring, I happened to be strolling through Stewart Park when I encountered Chue and some of his Hmong buddies with their bicycles. (You could buy a "used" bike for two dollars in the Stewart Park neighborhood.) The boys were gathered around a policeman who was talking to them. As I came up, the policeman was saying, "The next time I find a bike without a license, I'm going to impound it, understand?"

The black-haired heads nodded solemnly. Yes, yes, they

understood.

The policeman went away.

"Did you understand what he was talking about?" I asked.

They all shook their heads. No, not one of them had understood, but they had been too polite to admit it. So I explained what a license was and why it was needed.

"You need a license to ride a bike in America?" asked one boy, shaking his head incredulously. "I don't know that, I don't know that!"

When Chue's aunt and uncle moved from Minneapolis, he decided to stay and complete his high school education. At first he lived in an apartment with two other teen-age Hmong boys who were also in high school. However, their apartment was burglarized twice at night when the boys were home, and their car was stolen. So they moved out, and Chue got a room in the house of one of our Scout leaders, John VanValkenburg. When his part-time job wouldn't cover his rent plus other expenses, he called me on the telephone.

"Dave, what am I going to do?" he said. "I don't have any money."

I told him to move in with me, and he stayed until he graduated from South High. He worried about my irresponsible eating habits, though. When I would come in late at night, he'd be up in his room studying. Yet there was always some rice and chicken on the stove for me.

Chue became an Eagle Scout in Troop 100. For his special Eagle service project, he organized meetings for Hmong adults to help them learn how to speak English, read a city map, and make phone calls.

In 1984, Chue worked as a counselor at Camp Ajawah. He was put in charge of five young boys, all Americans. Although at fifteen he was five years older than his campers, he was still no taller than them. It made no difference; they idolized him. Once, when we were playing a softball game against our neighbors, Chue came up to bat. Someone started chanting "Chue Vue, Chue Vue!" and the whole camp picked up on it. Chue wound up and hit the ball so hard I doubt if it ever came down.

At the end of the two-week camp session, I presented Chue with the Camp Director's Award. In the citation, I said, in part, "In a camp made up of many groups and nationalities, Chue did the most to bring us all together by just being himself."

In 1987, Chue was runner-up in the Minnesota state high school speech contest. He spoke about the plight of his people and asked Americans for their understanding and support.

"History has proven that my people, the Hmong people, do not forget their promises," he said. "We, the Hmong people, will never forget that America is more than the home of the free. It is the source of our freedom. We will always remember that. That is my promise to you."

Kou Vue

Pao Nhia Vue

Toua Vue

CHAPTER FOURTEEN

KOU, PAO NHIA and TOUA VUE

I'm a student in the Minneapolis Public School and next year I'm going to the seventh grade. I feel that all of the Asian student still needs more help and so don't fire the bilingual aid because we all Asian student still needs it.
–Letter of Toua Vue to the Minneapolis School Board, 6/7/87

Kou Vue was born in 1970 in the Hmong town of Phak Khao in Laos. His family planted rice, corn, and vegetables and raised chickens, pigs, and ducks for the annual New Year's celebration. After two years, the family moved to Long Cheng, where Kou's father, Bee Vue, worked in a butcher shop owned by Kou's uncle. Kou's younger brother, Pao Nhia, was born in Long Cheng in 1972. Long Cheng was a busy place with an airport. Many American troups were stationed there. One night, the communists tried to take over the Long Cheng airport. An enormous amount of shooting continued through the night. Kou remembers watching tracer bullets like fireworks overhead. In the morning, there were dead enemy soldiers lying about. Angry citizens of Long Cheng had cut them up and driven cars over the bodies.

Kou's uncle eventually closed his butcher shop and went into the taxi business. The Vues then moved to Phak Khe to farm. The youngest Vue brother, Toua, was born at Phak Khe. Pao's first memory is of hearing Toua cry for the first time. He also remembers going out to farm with his father, taking food and blankets and spending long days and nights in the fields outside Phak Khe. There were some crazy dogs in Phak Khe, and Pao remembers huddling, terrified, behind a closed door as a mad dog roamed the streets.

From time to time, food was air-dropped by the Americans at a spot that was two hours' walking distance from Phak Khe. This was one way the Americans supported their Hmong allies and kept them fighting. Kou remembers hiking over to the drop site to pick up rice and canned beef. It wasn't as good as what the Hmong farmers raised, but in times of need it was just fine.

Almost every day, Kou walked for an hour to attend school. When he brought food along, he could eat it during the lunch period. Or he could buy food from little shops along the way. Sometimes, he had neither food nor money. Then he would run all the way home for lunch. He went hungry when the door at home was locked because he was too shy to ask anyone for help. There were no books at school, so everything had to be memorized. The teacher would stand pupils up in front of the class and tell them to recite yesterday's lesson. If a pupil didn't know it, the teacher would beat him with a ruler. If his fingernails were long or dirty, he was whipped. Kou doesn't remember learning anything in school, just hustling and bustling to avoid the whip and ruler.

One day, Kou and his brothers looked up into the sky and watched as massive flights of airplanes headed south. General Vang Pao, the Hmong chief, and all his forces were leaving the country. The war was over.

The communists who arrived at Phak Khe said they wanted to be friends with everyone, but things soon grew tense. People were afraid. They tried to follow Vang Pao, but the flights out of Long Cheng were booked solid. The communists were reportedly stopping cars and taxis bound for Vientiane. Some of the Vues' luckier relatives had gotten away, but being poor farmers, the Vues were left to fend for themselves. Their uncle brought his taxis to help them move to a city which was thought to be somewhat safer from the communist advance. The Vues moved on from here to a village near a place called Pha Deng, where they planted rice. Friendly neighbors gave them food to eat while their rice matured. Then, just as their rice was reaching knee height, airplanes appeared overhead and dropped leaflets instructing everyone to go and vote.

Bee Vue went into Pha Deng to vote. It was two days before he returned. When he came back, he told the family to pack up. The communists were taking over, and the Vues and other families decided to move out, leaving their rice to be harvested by others.

Thus began a life of running and hiding from airplanes. The group moved constantly. When they crossed a river, the planes dropped bombs. When they came to abandoned rice fields, they tried to harvest the crop at night. People fought each other for rice. They had very few animals, so there was little meat. Then the Hmongs got the idea to make salt from dirt. If you had salt, you had money, so they boiled the dirt and filtered it until they got salt. Though gritty and unclean, the salt was usable.

Kou remembers being very sick and hungry. The smell of cooking meat would cut through him and pierce his empty stomach.

Every day airplanes dropped bombs. The Vues tried to live in a cave, but the inside was evil and cold and made people sick. Kou and Pao found a hole in a cliff and began idly tossing rocks in to pass the time. They shouldn't have done this, for they had no idea what lurked in the depths of that hole. Whatever it was struck back that night. Asleep on his bed, Kou had a terrible dream. A blizzard of black and white whirligigs came spinning at him from out of the darkness. Then he was chased by two red devils. He couldn't run fast enough. He tried to disappear and come up in another place, but couldn't. He woke up sweating and feverish. Later, he and Pao got sick.

The Vues decided to try and move to Pha Hai, a place that lay hidden between two mountains. Perhaps the communists did not yet know of its existence. At Pha Hai there was nothing to eat and no place to plant rice. All the Vues became sick and took to their beds. Some people went back across a river to steal rice and corn from the fields around communist-controlled Pha Deng. This supplied them with what little food they had. But the communists soon began bombing Pha Hai.

Bee Vue decided to bring his family to live with relatives

in Kia Ma Na. It took them a week to get there, walking day and night without rest. They carried small children and heavy loads of rice and clothing. Soon the rice gave out and there was nothing to eat. Toua was sick and had to be carried. Kou and Pao walked barefooted, and the rocks in the pathway cut their feet. Kou's ankle became swollen and turned purple. He couldn't walk properly, but had to stumble on.

Near Kia Ma Na, they stopped to rest in a cattle shed, and the boys fell asleep immediately. When Kou awoke, his father had returned with some water and cabbage. Kou hadn't eaten for two days and remembers the delicious, fresh taste of the cabbage. They reached Kia Ma Na the next day.

On the other side of Kia Ma Na was a mountain and beyond that was an uninhabited forest. The Vues made this their home. Kou cleared the land with his father. They cut down trees and burned them. Once Kou slipped and tumbled down an ash-covered hill and got himself black with soot. The Vues planted rice and corn on the burned-over scar, and things started looking better as the crops came along. Then they were hit by a plague of grasshoppers. The insects were everywhere. Most of the crop was ruined. What was left was harvested and stored in huge cribs. Then rats attacked the cribs. Kou and his brothers stayed up at night, clubbing rats by torchlight. Since there was no other meat, they skinned the rats, cooked them, and made a feast.

After the New Year, the Vues planted more crops and prepared for their second year in this place. Kou was cutting bamboo with his father's big Hmong knife when the knife slipped and cut his hand to the bone. Since they had no medicine, his father cauterized the wound with hot coals and wrapped it in cloth.

Before Kou's wound had a chance to heal, the communists attacked Kia Ma Na from the air. The Vues fled once more, this time to a place called Pao La. There they worked in other people's fields, pulling weeds in return for something to eat.

But the communists were closing in on Pao La. Word came that the Hmongs would resist, so Bee Vue left to help in the defense. There was fighting one night. The boys could hear guns and see fireworks in the distance. The fighting came closer, so the Vues packed up and fled into the night.

The way led through a ravine choked with fallen logs and

swamp water, the overflow of a swollen river. Kou's sister, Pa, stumbled while carrying Toua, and they both sprawled headlong into the muck. They rose and kept going, unable to see in the darkness, but breaking branches and clearing a trail like so many stampeding elephants. Their faces, arms, and legs were cut, and their clothing torn to shreds. Kou remembered the dream he had during his sickness and his efforts to disappear. He ran all night.

At noon the next day the Vues came to a deserted farmhouse at the foot of a cliff in the village of Nu Thao. They changed clothes, built a fire to keep warm, and prepared a meal. Suddenly, a burst of gunfire erupted from the other side of the village. The family climbed the cliff and plunged into the bushes on top. They watched communist soldiers move through the village and invade the spot where they had left their food. The soldiers didn't climb the cliff, and the Vues crept away. At dusk they came to another farmhouse. Exhausted and hungry, they built a fire, cooked what little rice remained. Then they unrolled their blankets and slept at last.

The Vues returned to Nu Thao the following day. White flags of surrender were flying everywhere. The Vues realized they were at the end of their resources and it was time to surrender. They returned to Kia Ma Na. Their father rejoined them there after searching for them all over Mount Phu Bia. Having first hidden his gun, he had entered the communist-controlled areas and found them.

The Vues lived near Kia Ma Na for a year. Life was hard under communist rule, and soldiers were everywhere. Some were Vietnamese, some Pathet Lao, and still others were Hmongs from General Vang Pao's forces who had joined the enemy out of dire necessity. Nevertheless, the Vues managed to plant and harvest crops of rice and corn that year.

New Year's came and passed, and the Vues planted a second crop. When their rice had grown knee-high, the family had a visitor. Their mother's brother-in-law had returned from Thailand to show them the way out, and the Vues decided to attempt an escape. It was none too soon, for Bee Vue's brother Chue had already been taken away by the communists.

The Vues began gathering rice into the fields in preparation for the journey. One day they were stopped by Pathet Lao soldiers who demanded to know what they were doing. Bee Vue explained that they were simply going out to farm the fields, and the soldiers believed him. It was normal practice for the Hmong to spend several days at a time in the fields without returning home, so they would often bring rice and blankets with them. The soldiers let them go, and the Vues continued their stockpiling.

Preparations were finally completed. When it came time to go, several families left together. Packing the bundle he was to carry, Kou was beside himself with excitement and fear. The night was dark about them as they filed secretly into the forest. Kou could hardly see in front of his face. Hanging banana leaves formed strange shapes in the inky blackness. Nothing seemed real. Once, Kou stopped to wait for the line in front of him to move. Everything was deathly still. For re-assurance, he reached out to touch the person ahead of him. Instead he felt a cool, clammy banana leaf. Kou ran forward searching frantically for his family, and eventually stumbled headlong into them. They hadn't even missed him.

The Vues walked in the forest a week, day and night, avoiding trails. They drew gunfire at one point while crossing a path. Soldiers coming along the path must have discovered their footprints. They ran until the pursuit finally died away. In a few days it became safe to rest at night.They came upon a clear, shallow river containing many finger-sized fish. The men enjoyed shooting the fish with guns.

They continued for several more days, stopping each night. Other refugees joined them until they soon numbered perhaps fifteen hundred people, all driven by a desire to reach the safety of Thailand. They climbed rocky hills and descended into valleys. Sometimes they looked down upon a deserted one- or two-house village.

In one of the refugee families, there was an old grandfather who was too sick and frail to walk. One of his sons carried the grandfather on his back. But the burden was too great, and finally the old man asked his son to leave him in the forest. His family covered him with a blanket, gave him some opium, and went on without him.

There was much to carry. Bee Vue carried food and clothes, as well as his little son Toua, who was still not recovered from sickness. In addition, he carried bamboo poles. It was an overwhelming burden, and he staggered under the weight.

But he kept going.

At last they neared the Mekong River, all fifteen hundred of them, keeping as quiet as was possible for such a large group. On the top of a mountain, they came upon another group of Hmong refugees returning from a failed attempt to cross the river. This group had been turned upon by guides in search of money and opium. Some of their number had been shot and killed, while others were chased over a cliff to their deaths. The remnant was destitute and forlorn. The Vues gave them rice and left.

That night, as Kou tried to sleep, he could hear the distant sound of cars and trucks on the Thai side of the Mekong. He was beside himself with excitement, wondering how he would ever make it to the freedom and safety of Thailand. He stayed awake listening.

The next day, they climbed the last steep height before the river. Everyone carried bamboo to use for flotation on the river, making the going extremely difficult. They walked single-file now, watching for buried mines. At one point, Kou and Pao took a wrong turn. Thinking they were with the people ahead of them, they mistakenly followed a path that ended at a cliff edge. There were two dead bodies lying there. Far below in the distance the yellow-orange Mekong wound silently down from China and on to lands unknown. Beyond the river lay the sleepy fields and forests of Thailand. The boys turned and ran back to find the others.

The group ate lunch on the mountain, then made a late-afternoon descent toward the river. The body of a dead man lay rotting at the foot of the mountain. It stank, and flies were swarming about the mouth. Bee told his children not to look.

They passed through an area that was or had been a mine field. There were broken branches and bits of clothing scattered about the ground and clinging to bushes. They ran silently, in single-file, until they reached the base of a small rise. Somewhere beyond lay the river. They sat and rested as the sun set. Bee Vue went looking for fresh water to drink with their rice. He was gone more than four hours and Kou fell asleep waiting. When he awoke, it was the middle of the night. His father was back, and they made their last meal in Laos. Kou knew he had to eat, but he couldn't taste the food. Everyone was lost in his own thoughts.

It was time for the last dash to the water. The refugees split into three smaller groups, according to clan. The first two groups climbed the hill and disappeared. The Vues were in the last group. They waited, then climbed the hill in darkness. Just over the top was a road. They waited until a scout beckoned them to come. Then they dashed across. Somewhere off to their left was gunfire; the other groups were in trouble. Shooting increased, and they could hear people screaming for help. Panic seized the Vues' group as they ran. It was everyone for himself.

Kou ran with the others through a little lowland rice paddy. He crossed a wire fence and tore open the seat of his pants. The river appeared just ahead. Kou reached it and jumped in, but his bamboo life raft wouldn't hold him! What now? He climbed onto the bank and saw a Thai fishing boat waiting. He jumped in. Thai paddlers swung the boat around and headed away from shore, paddling furiously. Shooting continued downstream, and babies cried. Drowning people called out from the water. The night glowed and pulsated with light.

There were six people in Kou's boat: three Thai paddlers and three Hmong refugees. Kou didn't know any of them. When they reached midstream, the Thais stopped paddling and searched the Hmongs. They took seven silver bars from one old man. From Kou they got nothing. They paddled in toward shore and the Thais jumped out in knee-deep water, leaving the Hmongs in the boat to fend for themselves. Where were they? What side of the river were they on? They waded ashore, and more Thai people came down to the river's edge to check them for money. Wet and shivering, they found a road and followed it along the river. It led to some houses in a little fishing village. A woman came out of a house and built a fire for them. Kou stayed close to the younger man, who had known his father. He thought about his family and wondered if they were still alive. Finally, in spite of himself, he slept.

Back on the Lao shore, things had not gone smoothly. Kou's mother had reached the river, carrying Toua. She saw a fishing boat there and tried to jump into it, but missed and went sprawling into the water, dropping Toua and drenching both of them. By the time Bee pulled his wife from the river, the boat was already gone. Realizing that Pao and Kou were not with her, she went back to look for them. She found Pao. He had fallen into a hole and had been trampled. Now he was struggling with his bamboo raft, which was still stuck in the hole. Someone had tossed a dead baby onto the ground nearby. Kou was nowhere to be found.

Back at the river, Bee Vue was pleading with a Thai boatman. The boatman had a full load just now, but could he please come back for more people? He said he'd come back if there was no shooting and swung the boat away.

The Vues waited, huddled in the bushes on the riverbank. Off to their left, the shooting died away. The night became quiet again. Someone lit a cigarette lighter and held it up as a signal to the Thai boats. The hours passed. Soon it would be getting light. If the Thais didn't return, the Vues would have to run back to the mountain. They waited a little longer, and then some boats arrived.

Pao, Toua, their mother and a cousin got into one of the boats, while Bee and some other people boarded another one. The little canoe was so overloaded that it almost sank.

In midstream, the Vues were checked by Thai pirates. Everything was taken except their clothes. Toua was wearing a silver necklace that was ripped off his neck in a single tug. Only their mother was able to keep any money. She explained that her husband had all the money, and the ruse worked.

The Thais dropped them off, and they waded to shore. Thinking they were still in Laos, they ran and hid in some bamboo bushes. But then they heard their father's voice: "Everything's all right. This is Thailand."

Re-assembling on the riverbank, their first thought was: where is Kou? Had he survived? Had he been shot or drowned? They searched the riverbank. By the time they found him, it was already daylight. Kou was sound asleep next to the embers from the fire the Thai woman had built for him.

Their first need was food. The Thais had taken it all. They had had a pot full of rice, but the Thais had taken it, thinking there might be silver in the bottom. Now they had to go begging. Kou was starving. All he could do was lie there on the riverbank. The refugees who had just come across were all in the same fix. People sat around not knowing what to do. Babies cried. Late that night they ate a little rice.

The next day, police came from the city. They could get the refugees a truck for two hundred *baht*. Most of their money was gone, but some people had managed to keep a little.

That night another group tried to cross the Mekong. Kou heard the guns firing for what seemed like an eternity. No one made it across.

Some time during the night, a truck came, and the Vues rode on it to a lighted city. Kou hadn't seen electric lights since he had lived in Long Cheng long ago, but this was much more electricity than Long Cheng ever had. Pao had never seen electric lights.

The Vues lay on some grass for a night and a day. They were extremely hungry. Finally, an American brought food in a Toyota truck. There was no room in the Nongkhai camp, so they were bused straight to Ban Vinai, the Hmong refugee camp.

At Ban Vinai, the Vues asked permission to come to America. They'd been moving about for so many years now that they just wanted to live in a place where they wouldn't have to grab everything and run. They were afraid the communists would come to Thailand just as they had come to every other place the Vues had ever lived.

The transit camp in Bangkok where they stayed for a month was a house of horrors. It was a large building with cement floors. People camped in the halls. Toilets overflowed. The only way to take a bath or shower was to pour a bowl of cold water over yourself. Food was doled out daily to each family. There was no meat. The weather was hot and oppressively humid.

Kou and his brothers climbed up onto the roof of a building and watched airplanes come and go from the nearby Bangkok Airport until it was their turn to leave. Two months after arriving at Ban Vinai, the Vue family left for America.

When Kou started fifth grade at Field School in Minneapolis in the fall of 1980, he was shaking, and his heart was pounding. His teacher tried to explain something to him, but he didn't understand what she was saying. The American children laughed at his confusion. There was a Hmong girl in class, but Kou was too shy to ask her for help. When the class got up to go to another room, Kou didn't know what was happening or what he should do. Finally, he got together with another new Hmong boy named Kong Vang, and they helped each other.

Toua entered first grade. His cousin, Chengsheng Vu, was there to help him and explain things. Toua listened to the

American children speak English and wished he knew what they were saying. At lunch, the food was not anything he was used to. He ate some of it and started to throw the rest away when a woman began scolding him about something. He didn't know what she was saying, nor did Chengsheng. Finally they figured out that she was telling them to wipe the table off.

Pao, in third grade, was assigned a friendly American pupil as his guide. The boy showed him where to put his coat and how to raise his seat. He was Pao's first American friend, but soon the boy's family moved away.

The two older Vue brothers were among the first to join our Hmong Boy Scout Troop. There were two other Pao Vues in the Troop, but luckily they all had middle names, which is not always the case with Hmong boys. Pao was called Pao Nhia to distinguish him from Pao Ge and Pao Ly.

Toua joined the Troop a few years after his brothers. No one observing Toua Vue in action would guess that he'd ever had a single health problem in his life. At the 1987 Boy Scout Camporee, he won the physical fitness contest, popping off seventy-six consecutive push-ups. No one else came close.

Toua is in the seventh grade at Anwatin Junior High School in Minneapolis. He would have preferred attending Folwell Junior High, where many of his Hmong friends are students. However, he was doing so well in math that he was put in an accelerated program. He has gotten used to the new school by now and has four or five good buddies at Anwatin. None of them are Hmong.

Pao is known for his enormous strength. When we organized a Hmong judo team coached by John Holmes of the University of Minnesota, Pao and his friend Tria Thao became our champions.

Pao likes to fish. When we go camping, Pao and his friend Tria quickly find a river or lake where there might be fish. They sharpen sticks for spears and go wading around, searching the shallows, feeling beneath the rocks with their hands. No fish is safe when Pao and Tria are in the vicinity.

One day I took Pao and his friends to Taylors Falls, Minnesota, to climb the cliffs. I brought a climbing rope and tied myself in at the bottom to do the belaying. The climb was a demanding one, requiring tricky finger-and-toe holds. Not everyone could make it. Pao scampered up like a fly going up a wall.

When he finished the climb he commented, "I scared, but I just do my best."

We took some of our Scouts up to the Bois Brule River in northern Wisconsin to do some whitewater canoeing. As it drops toward Lake Superior, the Brule runs over a series of ledges that make it a challenge for anyone in an open craft. Pao was in the bow of my canoe. We took all the ledges in great style, Pao hollering with joy and excitement every time we went over one — except for the last drop. We were the tail-end canoe and as we plunged toward that final ledge, I could see everyone lined up, standing on rocks to watch us take it. There was an obvious chute right in front of the audience, but I decided to surprise them and go for an alternative drop a little to the left. I was wrong to try this and knew it as soon as I took a stroke of the paddle. The current was much too strong to fight. Spun sideways, we slid backwards through the chute, turned over and washed up on a shallow ledge below the drop where we righted ourselves. Over the din of the rushing water, I shouted to Pao, "You have to tip over once on a trip like this or you're just not running rapids."

Pao wants to get a good education. He wants to make something of himself and not "just hang around the street for the rest of my life." He says, "Kou and Toua are smarter than me. One of them will go to college. I'll have to find a job."

In the spring of 1985, when I was putting a summer-camp staff together, I realized I was going to need an assistant cook. I called around to various cooking schools and institutions. I made a long list and a short list and got nowhere. Then I remembered Kou Vue had a reputation as an excellent cook. One summer day the Camp Ajawah boys had been camping at Taylors Falls. We had put in a strenuous day rock climbing, hiking, and swimming. We straggled back to our tents tired and hungry. Before we could eat, however, we had to get fires going and food cooking. Just as we entered camp, a storm that had been threatening all day broke. Boys dove for their tents and it looked as if we might have a cold, wet, night without dinner. Then all over the campground, little cook fires appeared, bravely defying the elements. Each one was tended by a Hmong boy. I strolled over to a fire where Kou was busy with a pan of meat and stir-fried vegetables, oblivious to the rain which had thoroughly soaked his clothing. He greeted me cheerfully and offered me a spoonful. That evening we ate well and the Hmongs earned a respect resembling awe from their American buddies.

I took a chance and called Kou on the telephone. I told him I was looking for an assistant camp cook for the summer. Could he do it?

I expected some argument about not being able to cook American food, needing to earn more money, or having to attend summer school. Instead, without hesitation he said, "Dave, if you want me to do it, I will."

Kou and I shared a cabin at camp that summer and became good friends. Dan Hess organized a canoe race and insisted that I enter, so I recruited Kou, my roommate, to be my bow man. We set off into the wind on the quarter-mile course, paddling like maniacs and smashing into the oncoming waves. At the far buoy, I broke paddling stride long enough to jam in a powerful rudder and we hit the wind and waves just right for the turn. We did a nice pivot and came screaming back downwind like a fast freight. We had the best time and Dan gave us each a little birch-bark canoe that he had made as a trophy. I still have mine on my desk.

Kou was a good worker at camp. When summer ended, I asked Marcia Trelstad, the head cook, what she thought was the best thing about camp that year. She answered in two words: "Kou Vue."

In December, 1987, Kou and I made a quick trip to Texas to pick up my friend Mackenzie Brown and seven of his Lao Boy Scouts. Mackenzie had helped with the Hmong Troop in Minneapolis before he moved to Dallas. Now he was leading a Troop of Lao boys and wanted some of them to experience winter camping in the snowy, frozen North. So Kou and I made the trip to pick them up. The Lao stayed with us for a few days, camping with Hmong and American boys and having a blast in the snow. They had never really seen snow except for the kind that melts right away when it reaches the ground. We went cross-country skiing, sliding on mini-boggans, and had a couple mammoth snowball fights. We engaged in that most mysterious of all Minnesota sports, ice fishing. We slept outside under the stars. Friendships were made across ethnic barriers as the Hmong, Lao and Americans took to each other. The Lao especially looked up to the older Hmong leaders. They liked Kou.

After a week of fun, I drove the Lao boys back to Texas.

When Kou thinks about the future, he thinks about a responsibility to his family. His parents don't speak English and have a hard life in America. He must continue to look after their interests and set an example for his younger brothers and sisters. He sets a good example by his hard work, ambition, and striving for realistic goals. Kou will make it.

You Mai Chang

CHAPTER FIFTEEN

YOU MAI CHANG

Chang, You Mai, 55, of Mpls. Born in Xiengkhoaung Province, Laos. Arrived in America in 1980. Died Jan. 2, 1988 of heart failure. Survived by wife, Sai; sons, Sia, 32, Xiong Pao, 19, Yee, 16, Chan, 14, and Doua, 11; daughter, Khoua, 12; 6 grandchildren; brother, Nou Ying, 66, of St. Paul and sister, Yiv, in Laos. Farmer, village chief in Laos. Co-founder, member and past board member and secretary of Hmong & American Veterans Alliance. Member of Boy Scout Troop 100 Committee. Clan elder in Mpls. & St. Paul. Interpreter of Hmong tradition. Official player of *kheng* and other Hmong musical instruments. Visitation at White Funeral Home, 2730 Hennepin Ave., from 8 am Wed., Jan. 6th, until 1 pm Thur. Gravesite service at Lakewood Cemetery, 36th St. at Hennepin, 2 pm Thur.
—Yee Chang, Minneapolis Star Tribune, 1/6/88.

I arrived home late one evening from a holiday trip to Texas. My telephone message recording machine was blinking, indicating I had received some calls during my two-day absence. But, exhausted from driving, I went straight to bed without playing them back. Next morning I was putting on my suit and puttering around looking for my good shoes for church when the telephone rang. I picked up the receiver and heard my friend Bob Fulton.

"So you're back already," he said. "I was just going to leave a message on your machine. Have you heard what happened to You Mai Chang?"

"No."

"He died yesterday, about noon, of a heart attack."

"Oh, no!"

"Yee's really taking it hard. They're all taking it hard." Bob's voice broke. "I'm on my way over there now."

I hung up my receiver, saw the blinking light on the recording machine and turned it on. There was a message from Yee. His voice sounded far away. As he talked he gasped and struggled to catch his breath.

"Dave, this is Yee. I know you're not there but I just want to leave this message. We're in the waiting room at Hennepin County Hospital. My dad had a heart attack. He's in the emergency room now, and we're waiting for news. I just want you to know, and pray for him so he gets well." The message ended in a sob and a prayer, "Help me, Dave!"

Quickly, I found my shoes and drove through the bright, bitter cold of a Minnesota January to the Chang residence where the clan was already gathering. The tiny living room was jammed with Hmong people standing along the walls and sitting on folding chairs. In the center of the room was a table with bowls of rice and plates of meat. I found Chan and Khoua and some of the other children. Yee wasn't around. I was given a place at the table and sat down to eat some rice.

Then Yee entered the room. He was wearing a T-shirt which I had bought for him that fall on my visit to Thailand. On the shirt was a picture of the Temple of the Dawn in Bangkok, its towers soaring into a blazing red-and-yellow Asian sunrise.

I stood up and he came to me. "My dad's gone, Dave," he said, crying on my shoulder. I followed him up to his room, where some of his friends had gathered. With great difficulty, punctuated by gasps and sobs, he told me what had happened.

It was Saturday, about noon, and the family was preparing to attend a New Year's party. Suddenly, You Mai started choking. He could hardly breathe. An ambulance was called and arrived within minutes. But an attendant with a clip board insisted on official rigmarole. What was his name? How old was he?

"Can't you see he can't breathe?" Yee shouted at the attendants. " Do something so he can breathe."

You Mai was finally given oxygen and taken to the ambulance. Only one family member was permitted in the ambulance, and somehow Yee was elected. There was nothing Yee could do in the ambulance except hold his father's hand. Struggling for breath, You Mai Chang knew he was dying. He began reciting the debts that others owed to the family, so that Yee would know and be able to make an accounting. Yee tried to get him to be still and just breathe. You Mai took off his watch and gave it to Yee, and Yee tried to give it back.

At the hospital, You Mai was whisked away, and Yee was conducted to a waiting room. The family arrived soon after. No one was permitted to see You Mai. This was not the Hmong way, but it could not be helped. They had to follow the rules of this strange place. That was the point at which Yee called me. By the time I got to him, he had been crying for twenty-four hours straight.

"A lot of my friends lost their parents in Laos and Thailand," he continued. "But my dad got us all here safely, and I thought I had everything going for me. Now my whole life has collapsed. Who's going to help me now? Who can I run to when I need something? It feels like my root has been torn out.

He wanted to know you, Dave. Whenever you came over to the house, he set a chair for you and tried to talk to you. I tried to translate, but it was just too hard for him; he didn't know any English. He trusted you. That's why he let all of us, even Doua, go camping with you. He knew we'd be safe if we were with you."

Yee had loved and deeply respected his father, but he had never been close to him. They had never had much to say to each other. It was not the Hmong way for fathers to be close to their sons. Yee had never sat down and said to him, "I love you, Dad." But he had come to know his father by listening when You Mai talked to other people. In this way he had come to know a good man who was well liked and respected, a community leader whom people sought out for advice or just friendly talk.

A group of us drove to the funeral home to participate in the long, five-day and four-night Hmong funeral. The room where the casket lay was crowded with Hmong people of all ages. A drum was beating solemnly, majestically, and a *kheng*, the Hmong bamboo flute, sang its sad song. Yee put his arm around my waist and asked me to come bid his father goodbye.

We shouldered our way through the crowd, and when we got to the casket, Yee took his silver Eagle Scout pin out of his pocket and pinned it onto the lapel of his father's new suit.

For me, that was the start of a five-day celebration of the life of You Mai Chang. Some of the time I walked around the crowded room, or I would stand against the wall or sit in a chair. I drank whiskey from shot glasses that people poured and offered me in the name of the departed. Once or twice I joined in the ritual of kneeling and bowing in respect for the dead and in acceptance of his blessing. I met people I hadn't seen in years and made new friends. Now and then I saw an American face other than those of Scout leaders Dan and Tom Hess. Bob Fulton and Jane VanValkenburg were there also. Crowds of people commuted back and forth between the funeral parlor and the Chang home, where there was food and the chance for a little break. In Yee's room we played silly card games and caught some sleep on the floor.

Through it all, the drum spoke and the *kheng* sang. The drum said, "Give way, give way, give way. Step aside and let the spirit of a great man pass." And the *kheng* sang, "This way, this way, this way," leading the spirit back across space and time; to the shores of Hawaii, the teeming camps in Thailand, the dark, peaceful mountains of Xiengkhouang where You Mai was born– across the border into China from whence a hundred years ago the Hmong had fled the failure of their great uprising during T'ai P'ing times, across the Nan Shan Mountains and the gorges of the Yangtse and over great grasslands to some secret place in the unimaginable wastes of Mongolia whence the Hmong race had begun. There the ancestors of the Chang were gathered to receive their son.

On the last night of the funeral, I caught twenty minutes of sleep on the floor of the funeral home. I sat up all night and listened as the Chang and Yang elders recited the deeds of the departed. It was partly solemn, partly joyous, and partly corny. The whiskey flowed freely, there was laughter, elders made speeches — and I didn't understand any of it. But I was fascinated by it. I couldn't sleep and wanted more than anything to show my respect, so I sat cross-legged on the floor and listened until four a.m. Then I thought I had better get some sleep, since I was going to make an early morning journey. I went to get my jacket, rolled it up to use as a pillow, and lay down next to the wall with some other sleeping bodies.

I don't know if I even closed my eyes, but I had a terrible

dream. I was in the classroom lecturing. A student who had once given me trouble was there, and he wasn't paying attention. He had drawn his sweater up over his face and was apparently sleeping. In my dream, I stopped the discussion in mid-sentence and raged at him: "You there, listen to me! I'm talking to you!" In a transport of fury, I strode over to him, tore off the sweater and looked at his face. It was Yee.

At 4:20 I was nudged awake by the oldest Chang brother, Sia. "Dave, we have to go now," he whispered. At last it was time for me to make a small contribution to these ceremonies. Three cows were going to be butchered today in honor of the dead, and I had volunteered to find a truck and trailer to transport them, live, from the farm where they were purchased to the funeral home to be blessed and back to the farm again to be killed. I thought that was going to be easy to do. I would just call my friend Bucky Broadbent, a farmer of long experience who had grown up with me on Linwood Lake. We were the same age, and although we only saw each other every two or three years, we always seemed to have a lot to talk about.

Bucky was a big man around Linwood. People went to him for help and he always gave it freely, but he never seemed to be in any need himself. I thought he, if anyone, could find me a cattle trailer. But when I called him on the telephone he was away ice fishing in Canada and would not be back until later that evening. It was cutting things close if he wouldn't be able to help me, since a rig was needed the next day. I spent a lot of time on the telephone in the funeral home, trying to run down a cattle truck or trailer. I followed some leads that Bucky's wife Yvonne had given me. I called farmers and rental places, but nothing was available.

When evening came, I called the Broadbents again, and Bucky had just returned. Yvonne had already told him my story, so we chatted about snowmobiling and ice-fishing in Canada.

"Don't worry," Bucky said. "I can get you a trailer. You can use mine or I'll get somebody else's, because mine is a little big. It'll haul eight cows."

"Should I bring my van and a trailer hitch?" I asked.

"No, no. I have a truck you can haul it with. Just come up and get it. I'll figure out the best way to do it."

Now Sia was nudging me awake. It was the day after I'd gotten Bucky's rig. It was parked about a mile away, in the

Westminster Church parking lot, plugged into an electric outlet so it would be sure to start. Sia and I drove in his car through dark and empty streets in the grip of the coldest Minnesota January in three years. The temperature was far below zero, but Bucky's truck started, and we headed out into the countryside. We drove over icy roads for about an hour, just past the little town of Hugo.

There we stood at the kitchen door of a farmhouse, shivering in the cold. I wasn't dressed for the weather; my deep-winter clothes were all at home, where I hadn't been in several days. A few more minutes of this and I'd be dealing with frostbite, I thought. Sia, if anything, was in worse shape. Then a big-boned, strong-looking man who introduced himself as Larry soon opened the door and let us in. As he dressed, he scolded us for being so poorly clad. He led us out to the barn, and I sensed the healing powers of the searing cold. I backed the trailer into the barnyard and three energetic steers came pushing and stomping in. We went back to the house, and Sia counted out some seventeen hundred dollars onto the kitchen table. Then we drove home.

"You paid that farmer a lot of money," I said. "This funeral must be costing you a lot."

"Yes," said Sia, "but I have to do it for my father."

When we reached the funeral home, the cattle, never leaving the trailer, were dedicated, and I drove them back to the farm to be slaughtered. With me this time was You Mai's nephew, Blong Chang, who had been in America only one year. We both had a long, hard night, so we spoke very little. Behind us was the caravan of Hmong elders who would do the butchering. I wasn't sleepy, but fought physical and mental exhaustion as I struggled to concentrate on driving.

When I dropped the steers off, Larry, the farmer, spoke briefly with me.

"I understand you're the Hmong Boy Scout leader," he said.

"Yes," I replied. "One of the sons is our Senior Patrol Leader. We want everything about this funeral to work out right for them. Their father was a very important man to his community."

"Whenever the Hmongs buy three cows for a funeral, I know it's for a great man," said Larry. "It's only happened once or twice before."

I drove the empty rig back to Bucky Broadbent's farm where I sat in a friendly kitchen drinking coffee with Bucky and Yvonne. We talked about old times and old friends in the Linwood community and the changes we had seen. I was a kid over at Camp Ajawah when he was a farm kid pitching hay. Bucky knew a little about the Hmongs. One of his neighbors a couple of miles away was a Hmong family working a small farm. Bucky had helped them out a little when they needed to have their garden plowed.

"The Hmongs work hard," said Bucky. "Their children attend Linwood School, and they're all known as hard workers. They're good people."

"This family that's having the funeral is pretty good, too," I said. "Their father was a great man. He didn't speak any English and he didn't have a job, but the Hmong people came to him for advice and help. He was a lot like you, Bucky, in his own community."

I got my car, which had remained overnight in Bucky's barn, and drove back to the city. I stopped at Edison High School to pick up some of Yee's friends, and we headed to Lakewood Cemetery for the burial. We made it just in time.

But what about Yee? How was it with him during these five gruelling days? He was always present, sometimes busy, sometimes just sitting. He was there but he wasn't there. It was as if he were slowly slipping away, becoming more and more distant with each day. Having no central ceremonial role to play, he was just hanging around much of the time. During those five days he had passed rapidly through all the stages of grief, until, at last, he just sat, glassy-eyed, zombie-like, and numb; he was gone. The spirit had left him and was wandering lost somewhere, just as surely as his father's spirit was moving slowly toward its final resting place.

At the graveside it was announced that there was to be a feast directly afterwards at the Chang home for all who had participated in the funeral. When I got there, the tiny house was already crowded. Up in Yee's room with its Scouting pictures and memorabilia on the walls, his brothers, cousins and friends had gathered. The Hess boys, Bob Fulton, and Mike O'Neal were there. We sat around, ate rice and meat from tin plates, and talked. It should have been consoling. But where was Yee?

"Maybe he's with his girlfriend," said Charlie Chang, his cousin.

"That's all right, but he should be here. We need him here," I said.

Then one of the Hmong elders came in and invited us American elders to join his group downstairs. In the tiny living-room, a circle of chairs had been widened to include us. It was clear that the ceremonies were not quite over. Younger Hmongs were standing along the walls to watch and the women had crowded in from the kitchen. Yee's friends and brothers had followed us down from the upstairs room. Their faces were expectant, attentive. Then I noticed that Yee was there.

The ground rules for the ceremony were explained. The idea was that when your turn came, you were to say a few words, if you wanted to, down a shot glass of whiskey in one gulp if you wanted to, and pour a glass for the person on your left, who would do the same thing. If you didn't have anything particular to say or if you didn't want to drink, you could just pass. But clearly this was not going to be the moment to pass. With all eyes upon us, this was a rite that was going to have to be performed with style.

Just before the ceremony began, there was a brief discussion in Hmong, and Yee took a half-step forward. Now at last, Yee was going to have a significant role in his father's funeral. He would be interpreter.

The toasts began, not long, just a few words. They invoked the memory of the beloved You Mai, clan elder and family leader who had done so much to hold everyone together in their remarkable journey. They expressed a sense of loss and concern for his wife and children; thanked us Americans for taking time out from our busy lives, dropping everything and coming to do what we could. People listened and cried. Yee translated. Completely bilingual, he spoke softly but firmly and with confidence in both languages about the memory of "my dad" and about "my family". I could see that he was back with us again; he was Yee again, and in spite of my tears for the departed and his bereaved family, I rejoiced for the first time in five days.

When my turn came, I took the glass from Mike O'Neal. Suddenly I realized that I, too, needed to have a healing part to play, that I, too, needed to get back in touch with myself, and that this ceremony might help do it for me. I stood up. I was aware of Sai Yang, Yee's mother, handsome and regal, standing in the kitchen doorway. I spoke for her, and I spoke for Yee, and I spoke for everyone present. At first I had to struggle to get the words out, but after a while my voice steadied.

"As the leader of the Hmong Boy Scouts and on behalf of all these Americans here, I want to thank you for letting us be part of your ceremonies and for letting us celebrate the life of You Mai Chang with you. We are here because we share your sense of loss and concern for his wonderful family. You Mai was a great man. When a great man passes away, his passing tears a hole in the universe. And it tears a hole in all of our hearts, a hole that cannot be mended by each one of us acting alone. But you Hmong people have taught us Americans a way that it can be mended. We must do it together. We must stay together, support each other and always love each other. That way the hole in our hearts can be mended."

I drained the glass, sat down and poured a drink for Nhia Cha on my left. I had played my part. As Yee translated my words, the Hmongs in the room nodded and wept. When he had finished, I nodded to him my thanks. The toasting went on.

As the ceremony ended, Xeng Sou Yang stood up and announced that he had planned a New Year's celebration which had been postponed by the funeral. Now everyone was invited to his house for the party. We walked through crisp sub-zero night air to Xeng Sou's house and there was another table with rice and meat laid out. Again the youngsters and women crowded around to watch. Standing with his buddies was Yee, now just a good Hmong kid, no different from the others, watching these elders and perhaps thinking that he, too, someday, would be sitting at the table with them. As we took our seats, Mike O'Neal whispered to me, "Are we still in a funeral mode or are we in a New Year's mode?" It turned out we were to be in a lighter, New Year's mode. Again there was whiskey and toasting and, this time, laughter. When my turn came I was proud to be able to wish everyone a Happy New Year in the Hmong language.

Later, as we all walked back to Yee's house, Charlie Chang said to me, "Did you ever drink so much before, Dave?"

"Well, actually, Charlie, I was pouring it all down inside my shirt," I replied.

Up ahead, Yee was walking with the others, snuggled into

a coat Dan had lent him for the walk. He was talking and smiling a little. Now, perhaps, the healing process can begin for him, I thought.

Scoutmaster
David L. Moore

CLOSER FRIENDS NOW

I know that my parents and friends are not here with me,
but I am sure they would be proud of what I have done and
what I want for the future.

—*Chue Yongyuan Vue*

Ontario, Canada
August 25, 1987

The distance from Elbow Lake into Eva appeared long on the map, and in fact, no portage was indicated. We just figured there would probably be a trail. We were right. We landed and loaded up, and I swung the canoe onto my shoulders. With any luck this would be our last portage.

The trail was long, with many ups and downs. At first I thought I was in the lead, but then I realized Yee was carrying a canoe just ahead of me. He would stop to rest, but every time I approached, he'd lift his canoe and keep going. We slogged through mucky places, clambered over rocks, and crossed a small stream. Yee set the pace ahead of me, and I couldn't catch him. My portage yoke was coming off, so I held the canoe onto my shoulders, adjusting it with every step. Alvin, following close behind, helped me get under a log. How had Yee squeezed through there on his own?

To make the distance endurable, I let my thoughts wander. I thought about my Hmong Boy Scouts and their long journey. Yee would be a senior at South High in Minneapolis in the fall. Some of the others were a little further along, having maintained the Hmong tradition of marrying young.

Vang Yang, once so pampered by his sisters, was married and had two children of his own. Xe Vang, who spent a year and a half in a prison camp, then lost his parents, was married with a two-year-old son, Sue Vang. He was a receptionist in the office of a Vietnamese doctor who worked mostly with Hmong people. Neng Vang, who was wounded and lost much of his eyesight, had no job, but he was married with three fine children. Xeng Lor, who had left his father in camp at Ban Vinai, was married before his term as Senior Patrol Leader expired. He had four sons. The oldest, Peter, an American citizen by birth, would be old enough to become a Boy Scout in 1993. Chao Lee, who was wounded and left for dead, was married.

Yeng Vue and Chue Hang worked in Minneapolis. They had not yet married. Chue was a good mechanic who could fix everything from bicycles to automobiles. He had graduated from high school and was working as a stock-boy. He wanted to finish his education. After that he might think about getting married.

I thought I'd never again see little Blong Xiong, who became homesick at Camp Ajawah, then moved away to Duluth. But one day he turned up right under my nose. I saw the name Blong Xiong on a list of ninth graders at Edison High School, where I taught. I looked up his schedule and tracked him down. He was the same Blong I had known, but he was completely transformed. I met a polite, quiet, studious young man with a friendly smile. Yes, of course he remembered me. We talked for a few minutes and resolved to keep in touch. A little later, he attended one of our Scout meetings. Yee remembered him right away, and they talked about their old times at camp. Now Blong was with us once more.

Some of my Scouts were now college students. Pao Ly Vu was attending the University of Minnesota, Su Thao was a third year student at Augsburg College, Chue Vue attended Jamestown College, and Kou Vue attended Winona State College. If they had stayed in Laos, these boys would all be married by now with families to care for. But they were adopting some of the ways of their new homeland. Some day they would be the spearhead of change, hope, and success for the Hmong people.

In the summer of 1988, I drove Kou Vue down to Winona State University for his freshman orientation and test-taking. As always, he was totally organized and knew exactly what he was doing. He didn't need me, but was glad to have me there for support. I attended some parents' meetings and hung around while he took his tests. Then we had dinner and went over to the student union to play some pool. We played a couple of games, each winning one. I said goodbye, gave him the keys to my car so he could use it for a couple of days, and returned home on the Amtrak.

In that same year, Chue Vue won a scholarship to Jamestown College in North Dakota. I drove him there that fall. As we motored across the flat Dakota plains, the shock of isolation began sinking in. Chue just looked out the car window, shook his head, and kept repeating, "Boy, oh boy." We drove into Jamestown, a quiet, tree-lined, settled-looking town, found a Chinese restaurant and had a last meal of rice and chicken. We talked about our scouting adventures over the years. I told Chue that if he could survive until Thanksgiving, he could survive anything. The irony of giving survival advice to Chue Vue was not lost on me. I spent the night in his dorm room, and in the morning we shook hands. He gave me a last friendly smile before I left.

Now I staggered under the weight of my canoe and almost slipped. Suddenly there was Yee, walking back-free without a canoe. He was soaked in sweat, but grinning at me; first over the portage.

"You're tough, Yee, you're tough," I said.

I set my canoe down on the rocky edge of a crystalline lake. We returned and helped the others until everyone was together at last. No more portages! We jumped into the water to cool off. We ate a lunch of chocolate, and Yee shared the Ryekrisp he had saved from breakfast. When we finished, we loaded up our canoes and shoved off for the last time, navigating back toward civilization across the huge, glassy-smooth surface of Eva Lake.

August 26

I was homeward-bound with the Hmongs. Yee was at the wheel of the van, and I was slumped in the passenger seat. There was a lot of talk in the Hmong language behind me.

Camp was over. The canoe trip was over. Summer was over. It was the time of year when everything comes to an end. Old friends say good-bye and disappear forever. Old moorings give way, and old, secure statuses change. An empty mood was on me, and I couldn't shake it. I was slowly slipping away.

"Did you enjoy your trip, Dave?"

Yee had sensed my mood and was trying to reach out and haul me back. We talked about the canoe trip just past. It had been a good trip. The adversities had brought us together and made us support one another. With no outside resources, we had to rely solely on ourselves — our strength, our initiative, our daring. We had all grown a little stronger and more confident. We were closer friends now.

We drove on through darkness. Along about Silver Bay, I took over driving. One by one my passengers fell asleep. Yee too fell asleep, and I drove on in silence.

At last we reached the city. I drove up and stopped in front of Yee's house. He stirred and began collecting his baggage.

"Well, so long, Yee. I really liked working with you this summer," I said.

"I liked working with you, too, Dave."

Yee smiled, slung his pack onto his shoulder, walked up to the door and was gone.

CHRONOLOGY

The stories of the boys in Boy Scout Troop 100 are clearer when seen in a wider historical perspective. The following dates and events are enlightening.

About B. C. 2500: The Hmong begin to migrate into China from their Mongolian homeland.

B. C. 214: The Hmong of south central China are conquered by the Ch'in dynasty. The Hmongs' millennia-long struggle for freedom from the Chinese begins.

1600's : The first Europeans to make contact with the Hmong are French Catholic priests. They are surprised to find the Hmong to be a gentle and generous people, contrary to Chinese descriptions of them as blood-thirsty barbarians.

1700's: At least four major rebellions of the Hmong against China's Manchu dynasty are crushed.

1776: The Hmong king, Sonom, is tricked into surrendering to the Chinese. He and his family die bravely and defiantly under torture.

1810's and 1820's: Some of the Hmong begin to migrate into

Laos seeking empty uplands in which to cultivate opium.

1855 to 1881: The Hmong of south China engage in a prolonged rebellion in conjunction with the Panthay and T'ai P'ing rebellions. They are defeated and slaughtered in great numbers. Their exodus to Indo-China begins.

1880's: The Hmong in greater numbers and the French move into Laos at the same time, each for different reasons. They make common cause.

1893: Laos becomes a French protectorate.

1896: The Hmong rebel against the French in protest against the French discriminatory taxation policy.

1917 to 1922: "War of the Insane": Major rebellion of the Hmong against the French ends with the assassination of its leader, Pa Chay.

1934: Mao T'se-tung, leading communist forces on the Long March across China, discovers the Chinese Hmong in the mountains of Kweichow province. Many of the Hmong join Mao's march to northern China. They are especially useful in the mountain fighting that Mao is forced to conduct against the Nationalist forces.

1941 to 1945: World War II. Touby Lyfoung, the Hmong chief, supports the French. Fay Dang, another chief, supports Japan.

1945: Japanese occupation of Laos is opposed by King Sisavang Vong and the patriotic elements of Laotian society.

1946: France regains control of Laos. War begins between French forces and independence movements which are increasingly dominated by communists forces in Vietnam, Cambodia and Laos.

1950: The United States recognizes Laos as an "Associated State within the French Union." French reverses in Indo-China lead them to abandon most of northern Vietnam to the communist

Vietminh.

1953, March: Seven thousand Vietnamese regulars invade Laos. They begin to surround the strategic Plain of Jars in the Hmong heartland, where the French and Touby Lyfoung, the Hmong political chief, are dug in. Hmong guerrillas cut the Vietnamese supply lines, and the Vietnamese retreat.

1954, April: Dienbienphu is beseiged. A French army is trapped and surrounded in communist-held territory on the Laos border of Vietnam. Four hundred Hmong "special commandos" from Laos, led by Lieutenant Vang Pao, are too late to raise the siege.

May 8: Dienbienphu falls, ending the French presence in Indo-China. Vietminh forces, flushed with victory, invade Laos in support of the Laotian communist Pathet Lao. The Royal Lao Government moves to pacify the Pathet Lao, while at the same time keeping in being a three thousand-man force of French-trained Hmong guerrilla soldiers as insurance against a communist coup.

May to July: Four-Power Geneva Conference on Indo-China (which actually began before the fall of Dienbienphu) leads to an armistice and French recognition of the independence of Vietnam, Cambodia and Laos. An extremely fragile "peace" covers a clandestine power struggle by indigenous forces. The United States begins to be interested in keeping Laos from falling to the communists.

1955: Laos is admitted to membership in the United Nations.

1956: The United States signs a treaty of economic cooperation with Laos.

1959: The Royal Lao Government forms a coalition with the communist Pathet Lao.

1960, August 9: Captain Kong Le of the Royal Lao Army takes over the government in Vientiane in a coup, establishing a neutralist government, but inviting the communists to join him in a coalition. This is the beginning of a prolonged three-cornered struggle that will last for several years between neutralists, communists and rightists.

December 16: Rightist General Phoumi Nosavan drives Kong Le and the communists out of Vientiane in bloody fighting. Kong Le retreats north.

December 31: Kong Le seizes the Plain of Jars in the Hmong heartland with Pathet Lao help. Russian Ilyushin bombers from North Vietnam drop paratroopers onto the Plain. Lieutenant Colonel Vang Pao, Hmong chief and loyal officer in the Royal Lao Army, is defeated and conducts an orderly retreat to Padong in the mountains south of the strategic plain, where he sets up headquarters. Meanwhile, Sam Neua City, key to far northern Laos, has fallen to the communists.

1961, January: President John F. Kennedy decides to support the Hmong and send special forces to Laos. He sends Green Beret instructors to Laos to train Hmong special forces at Padong. The "Secret War" for the Plain of Jars, key to control of all Laos, begins and lasts until 1975 and beyond. The C.I.A. begins the covert build-up of Hmong General Vang Pao's guerrilla forces to fight the Pathet Lao and Vietminh. Hmong mountain villages ringing the Plain have become unsafe due to Pathet Lao and neutralist infiltration of the area. To protect themselves, they send recruits to fight in Vang Pao's army. With too few men left for farming, these Hmong villages must rely on the United States for rice drops. America also provides money, schools, medicines, and military protection. Helicopter and airplane landing strips are built in many of the villages. A Great-Power confrontation over Laos is shaping up.

March 23: In a news conference, President Kennedy stresses the importance of Laos.

March 31: Laotian Premier Prince Souvanna Phouma calls for a fourteen-nation conference to restore peace in Laos.

May: Vang Pao, driven out of Padong, retreats southwest to Phak Khao. His army is accompanied by nine thousand Hmong women and children who experience massive casualties on the march.

June 3 to 4: President Kennedy and Soviet leader Nikita Khrushchev, meeting in Vienna, call for a neutral Laos.

July: As a fragile truce emerges, the United States is

secretly arming a Hmong force under Vang Pao which in time will grow to an eighteen thousand-man Hmong army.

December: Vang Pao moves his headquarters to Long Cheng, a natural mountain stronghold more easily defensible than Phak Khao, where he establishes a military base, and to Samthong, where he locates a refugee center for civilians. In the course of a few years, Long Cheng will become one of the busiest airports in the world. Between 1969 and 1972, an airplane will take off or land approximately every three minutes.

1962, July: Fourteen-nation conference on Laos is held in Geneva, with Laotian independence and neutrality guaranteed. A Great-Power confrontation is thus defused. The United States pulls all overt military personnel out of Laos. But the Secret War continues.

1963: In and around the Plain of Jars sporadic three-cornered fighting goes on between communist Pathet Lao, Kong Le's neutralists, and Vang Pao's forces.

1964, May: A major battle rages for the Plain of Jars. The Pathet Lao turn on Kong Le, who asks Vang Pao to help him. He is nevertheless driven off the Plain. Operation Barrel Roll, the secret American bombing of Laos, begins. The number of tons of bombs dropped on the Plain of Jars alone between 1968 and 1972 will exceed all of the tonnage dropped anywhere by the United States in all of World War II. Caught in the middle of this holocaust are the Hmong, their homes and families. Almost every Hmong male between the ages of fifteen and fifty is in Vang Pao's army. Some are considerably younger than that.

August: The Gulf of Tonkin incident will result in massive escalation of American forces in Vietnam. Laos — and the Hmong — will feel the impact of that escalation.

1965: United States combat troops are introduced into Vietnam. Systematic bombing of North Vietnam begins. In Laos, Long Cheng and Phou Pa Thi, Hmong mountain strongholds, become radar relay centers in support of the American air operation over Vietnam. Hmong guerrillas are regularly sent to rescue

American pilots downed in Vietnam.

1966: Sam Neua City, key to far northern Laos, falls to the Pathet Lao.

1968, January: Battle for Phou Pa Thi, mountain-top air tracking station, rages. Vang Pao's forces are bled white and driven off in defeat after savage fighting. Hmong morale sags. The highway of invasion from Vietnam into the Hmong heartland appears to be open. Vang Pao's army is now largely made up of old men and boys.

> **October 31**: The United States election-eve bombing halt over North Vietnam releases American bombers for duty in Laos on a gigantic scale.

1969: United States Senate bans United States armed intervention in Laos — but the Secret War goes on.

> **August to September**: In a last-ditch, desperate effort to stem the communist tide, the United States air-drops Hmong paratroopers onto the Plain of Jars, which they capture after savage fighting. The communist forces have made a strategic retreat, leaving the Plain all but deserted.

1970: With the onset of the dry season in February, everyone knows that the Pathet Lao will try to regain the Plain of Jars. Nor are the Hmong sanctuaries to the southwest of the Plain safe. The civilian air evacuation of Samthong and Long Cheng is begun. Long Cheng itself is threatened. Vang Pao orders every available Hmong male age fifteen and older into his army. The Plain of Jars is overrun by the Pathet Lao. On March 6, Samthong falls and is totally destroyed. Long Cheng comes under periodic bombardment and attack. Half of Vang Pao's forces are wiped out just trying to hold on. Then come the rains.

1971, March: By this time some Hmong are migrating down out of the northern mountains into the lowlands north of Vientiane, where they exist in squalid refugee camps.

1973: A cease-fire in Laos is declared. The United States makes a last bombing sortie.

1974: A coalition government and political council formed in Vientiane establish new policies for the future of Laos. Touby Lyfoung, chief of the Hmong, is in the cabinet. He tries to make contact with Fay Dang, the Hmong communist leader. It is too late.

1975, April: Cambodia falls. South Vietnam falls.

May 9: The Pathet Lao newspaper announces, "It is necessary to extirpate, down to the root, the 'Hmong' minority."

May 12: Vang Pao toys with the idea of attacking and seizing Vientiane in order to carry on the war. Yang Dao, a Hmong member of the Royal Lao government, dissuades him on the ground that such an attack would be suicidal.

May 14: Vang Pao, realizing tht everyone has abandoned the Hmong, including the Americans and the Royal Lao government for which he fought so long, leaves for Thailand. Long Cheng falls. The Hmong begin their exodus from Laos. Yang Dao, who cannot get an airplane to take him from Long Cheng to Vientiane, makes the trip by automobile. He is stopped several times at communist check-points, but manages to bluff his way through.

May 15: Yang Dao and thirty-five members of his family leave for Thailand.

August: Vientiane falls.

December: The monarchy is abolished, supplanted by the People's Democratic Republic of Laos.

1975 to 1978: The Hmong make their last stand on Mount Phou Bia. They finally succumb to bombs, artillery, napalm, gas and chemicals.

BIBLIOGRAPHY FOR THE CHRONOLOGY

Burchett, Wilfred G. *The Second Indo-China War; Cambodia and Laos*, New York: International Publishers Co., Inc., 1970.

Hendricks, Glenn L., Bruce T. Downing and Amos S. Deinard, eds., *The Hmong in Transition*, New York: The Center for Migration Studies of New York, Inc., 1968.

Langer, William L., ed., *An Encyclopedia of World History*, Boston: Houghton Mifflin Company, 1968.

McCoy, Alfred W., *The Politics of Heroin in Southeast Asia*, New York: Harper & Row, 1972.

Mottin, J. *History of the Hmong*, Bangkok, Thailand: Odeon Store Ltd. Part., 1980.

Quincy, Keith. *Hmong; History of a People*, Cheney, Washington: Eastern Washington University Press, 1988.

Robbins, Christopher. *The Ravens; the Men who Flew in America's Secret War in Laos*, New York: Crown Publishers, Inc., 1987.

Schanche, Don. *Mr. Pop*, New York: David McKay Co., 1967.

Stevenson, Charles A. *The End of Nowhere; American Policy toward Laos since 1954*, Boston: Beacon Press, 1972.

Additional sources for chapter epigraphs

Yee Chang– Taken from Ernest E. Heimbach, *White Hmong-English Dictionary*, Data Paper #75, Southeast Asia Program, Cornell University, Ithaca, New York, August, 1969, p. 462.

Xe Vang– Col. Henri Roux of the French special forces, 1945, quoted in *La Fabuleuse Aventure du Peuple de l'Opium* by Jean Lartguy with the collaboration of Yang Dao, Presses de la Cite, 1979.

Yeng Vue– *The Brave Woman and the Tiger*, from Charles Johnson, ed., *Myths, Legends and Folk Tales from the Hmong of Laos*, Macalester College, 1985, p. 403.

Closer Friends Now– Chue Vue, *Collected Works of Chue Yongyuan Vue*, Primus Law Office, p. 23.

Other Pertinent Readings

The following provide background on life in Southeast Asia in the middle and latter 1950's. The first two describe conditions in Vietnam from an American doctor's viewpoint; the third deals with northern Laos. While he does not name the Hmong in any of them (he refers to them instead as the Meo), the war was, in time, to engulf them as it had the tribes Dooley lived among.

Dooley, Thomas A., *Deliver Us From Evil,*   1956.

Dooley, Thomas A., *The Edge of Tomorrow,* 1958.

Dooley, Thomas A., *The Night They Burned The Mountain,* 1960,   published as *Dr. Tom Dooley's Three Great Books,* New York: Farrar, Straus & Company, 1960.

FROM CAT'S-PAW PRESS...

Roughing It Elegantly: A Practical Guide To Canoe Camping, by Patricia J. Bell. Enjoy North America's finest canoe wilderness elegantly—simply, efficiently, and with style. Shows how anyone can safely and comfortably enjoy a wilderness experience.

It's a planner! It's a log!
The Paddler's Planner, by Patricia J. Bell, makes it easier for the camper to rough it elegantly — efficiently, simply and with his or her own style.

ORDER FORM

Cat's-paw Press
9561 Woodridge Circle
Eden Prairie, MN 55347

Please send me _____ copy (copies) of **Roughing It Elegantly: A Practical Guide To Canoe Camping,** by Patricia J. Bell, (ISBN 0-9618227-1-6). I am enclosing $9.95 (plus $.60 sales tax, if in Minnesota) and $1.50 for shipping for each copy.

Please send me _____ copy (copies) of **The Paddler's Planner** (ISBN 0-9618227-3-2).I am enclosing $12.95 (plus $.78 sales tax, if in Minnesota) and $1.50 for shipping for each copy.

NAME _____

ADDRESS _____

_____

_____

Please autograph the book to :_____

FROM ST. JOHN'S PUBLISHING...

Parenting a Business, by Donna L. Montgomery, looks at business relationships from a parenting standpoint.

Surviving Motherhood, by Donna L. Montgomery. A look at family relationships written by a mother of eight who is a survivor of motherhood herself.

Kids+ Modeling= Money, by Donna L. Montgomery, is all you need to help your child begin a rewarding and prosperous modeling career. Discover the secrets of modeling success.

ORDER FORM

St. John's Publishing
6824 Oaklawn Avenue
Edina, MN 55435

Please send me _____ copy (copies) of **Parenting a Business** (ISBN 0-938577-04-2).I am enclosing $14.95 and $1.50 for shipping for each copy.

Please send me _____ copy (copies) of **Surviving Motherhood**, (ISBN 0-938577-00-X). I am enclosing $6.95 and $1.50 for shipping for each copy.

Please send me _____ copy (copies) of **Kids+ Modeling= Money,** (ISBN 0-13-515172-4).I am enclosing $9.95 (hardcover) and $1.50 for shipping for each copy.

NAME _____

ADDRESS _____

_____

_____

Please autograph the book to : _____